I0583570

JEAN LORRAIN

MONSIEUR DE BOUGRELON

AND OTHER STORIES

TRANSLATED AND WITH AN INTRODUCTION BY

BRIAN STABLEFORD

THIS IS A SNUGGLY BOOK

Translation and Introduction Copyright © 2020
by Brian Stableford.
All rights reserved.

ISBN: 978-1-64525-035-7

MONSIEUR DE BOUGRELON
AND OTHER STORIES

"JEAN LORRAIN" (1855-1906) was the pseudonym of Paul Duval, adopted at the insistence of his father, a Norman ship-owner, who wanted to protect the family name from the disgrace of employment by a poet. A flamboyant homosexual dandy, when forced to make a living from his pen after his father died ruined, he became one of the most prolific and highest-paid journalists of the *fin-de-siècle*, and the personification, in his lifestyle as well as his writing, of the Decadent Movement. *Monsieur de Phocas. Astarté* (1901; tr. as *Monsieur de Phocas*), compounded out of numerous short stories, is a kind of retrospective summary of the Decadent world-view, written after he was forced to leave Paris because of health problems occasioned by his use of ether as a stimulant, which did not take long to kill him thereafter.

BRIAN STABLEFORD'S scholarly work includes *New Atlantis: A Narrative History of Scientific Romance* (Wildside Press, 2016), *The Plurality of Imaginary Worlds: The Evolution of French roman scientifique* (Black Coat Press, 2017) and *Tales of Enchantment and Disenchantment: A History of Faerie* (Black Coat Press, 2019). In support of the latter projects he has translated more than a hundred volumes of *roman scientifique* and more than twenty volumes of *contes de fées* into English. He has edited *Decadence and Symbolism: A Showcase Anthology* (Snuggly Books, 2018), and is busy translating more Symbolist and Decadent fiction.

SNUGGLY BOOKS

CONTENTS

INTRODUCTION

MONSIEUR DE BOUGRELON, by Jean Lorrain, was originally published as a series of eleven short pieces, under the heading "Contes au trois Ubus (car ils sont trois)" [Tales for the Three Ubus—for there are three] in the daily newspaper *Le Journal* between 20 January and 10 May 1897, all eleven episodes beginning on page one of the newspaper. The entire text was reprinted by Édouard Guillaume of the Librairie Borel as an illustrated book in the "Lotus Bleu" series later the same year. The supplement translated here as an Epilogue was published with that description in the 15 June 1935 issue of *Les Nouvelles littéraires* and then added to the text of the novella in an edition published by Éditions Arc-en-ciel in 1944. Although the supplement was written in January 1898, as the text makes clear, it was not published then, perhaps being rejected by *Le Journal*, or perhaps never even submitted because the author considered it too idiosyncratic or too personal. It clearly does not belong to the original text, but it does add something significant to it, in terms of casting further light on what the story meant to its author; it represents a rare instance of an author confessing that one of his characters continues to haunt him, some time after the publication of the work for which he was invented, in the fashion of an exotic species of phantom to which only writers can be subject.

The other nine stories included in the collection are taken from the posthumous collection *Du Temps que les bêtes parlaient: Portraits littéraires et mondains*, published by the press associated with the *Courrier français* in 1911,[1] six of which had first appeared in *Le Journal*; "Le Chat de Babaud Monier" was in the 4 June 1903 issue, "Le Perroquet de Madame Germont" in the 10 June issue, "Hoguemore" in the 23 June 1903 issue and "Les Oies de Pirou" in the 16 June 1903 issue. Those four stories constituted the series "Du Temps que les bêtes parlaient" as headed in *Le Journal*. They were directly followed in the paper by two stories headed "Du Temps des belles dames," "Le Partie de volants," in the 27 June issue and "Une Partie de campagne" in the 4 July issue, but that heading was then abandoned in the newspaper, although the 1911 collection, which uses it as a subheading, added four more items to it, only one of which had previously appeared in *Le Journal*, in a somewhat different version: "Tas-de-Foin," which adapts a story published in the 20 April 1902 issue of *Le Journal* as "La Femme au tigre." The nickname Tas-

---

1 Numerous references on the world wide web give the date of the collection as 1900, but that is obviously mistaken, copied blindly, like many other items of misinformation; although the book itself is undated, 1911 is definitely correct as the date of its publication.

de-Foin, which provides the title of the revised version, does not appear in the original version, and almost all the other names employed in the story are changed.

It is not obvious who made the alterations to "La Femme au tigre" to produce the new version, or when, although it is possible that Lorrain revised the story for intended book publication while he was still alive, but that the revised version was not used at the time. If so, it might be the case that the more drastic alterations that produced "Une vieille histoire" (tr. herein as "An Old Story") which is a revised version of one of Lorrain's earliest short stories, published as "La Marquise Hérode" in the 2 October 1887 issue of the *Courrier français*, were also his. The first third of the original story is cut and replaced by a much shorter section likening the central character to the eponymous anti-heroine of Catulle Mendès' novel *Mephistophéla* (feuilleton 1889; book version 1890). "Fleur de banlieue" (here tr. as "Flowers of Suburbia") had appeared only a year earlier in another posthumous collection of Lorrain's work, *Les Pelléastres* (1910), but I cannot locate any publication of the story during the author's lifetime.

The remaining item included in the "Du Temps des belles dames" subsection of the 1911 book, "L'Horreur du simple," is not included in the present collection because it has been translated previously, as the first half of a story entitled "Madame Holland" in the collection *Fards et poisons* (1903; tr. as *Fards and Poisons*), a story apparently included in that collection to replace "Victime," which had had to be dropped when it became the subject of a lawsuit. It might be the case that the editor of the 1911 collection did not realize that it had been previously published in a book, and that he was also unaware of the previous appearance of "Fleurs de banlieue," because *Les Pelléastres* was issued by another publisher, who might have acquired a different manuscript independently.

In order to understand *Monsieur de Bougrelon*, and to understand why its protagonist continued to haunt the author for some time after it was finished, it is necessary to see it in the context of the literary endeavor of the day, and that of the precise juncture at which Jean Lorrain's career had arrived at the beginning of January 1897, in terms of the way he saw himself, his past and his probable future. Although he was not yet forty-two years old, and he recently had become one of the highest-paid journalists in Paris, he was almost certainly aware that his career was entering a phase of decline, partly because the calendar was inexorably counting down to the terminus of the *fin-de-siècle*, of which he was not merely a chronicler but a kind of self-appointed incarnation. He was also painfully aware that he was seriously ill; his gut had been badly ulcerated in the late 1880s when he began using ether as a stimulant, and although a section of his intestine had been removed in 1893 by the famous surgeon Samuel Pozzi—who continued to treat him throughout the rest of his life—the problem had not been overcome.

Monsieur de Bougrelon, which had a very wide, if intermittent, circulation by virtue of the publication of its sections in *Le Journal*—for which Lorrain had been working regularly since 1895—was hailed by some contemporary critics as a literary masterpiece, and that assertive defense was probably necessary, as it is undoubtedly one of the most peculiar works ever to appear in a newspaper, even though *Le Journal* had literary pretentions considerably more elevated than rival dailies. It is unusual both thematically and stylistically, far more experimental than the shorter stories that Lorrain had been contributing in some abundance to contemporary daily newspapers, or the novelettes that he occasionally published in monthly periodicals.

Although *Monsieur de Bougrelon* is in some ways a derivative work, inspired in some measure by Georges Rodenbach's *Bruges-la-morte* (1892) and transfiguring motifs and passages from other Decadent works, its eponymous "hero" is an extraordinary invention, considerably distanced from one of the models from which the character-portrait is drawn, Jules-Amédée Barbey-d'Aurevilly (1808-1889), and remarkably exotic even by the standards of an era in which the intersection of neo-Naturalist and Symbolist Movements had created an intense interested in abnormal psychologies. That actual individual that Lorrain had once known was, however, not the character's only model; the collective title of the eleven "*contes*" making up the whole relates the character directly to the protagonist of *Ubu roi*, the play by Alfred Jarry that had, notoriously, opened and closed on 10 December 1896, at whose only performance Lorrain had surely been present.

Monsieur de Bougrelon is evidently, at least to some extent, Lorrain's Ubu: a character who addresses his audience provocatively in a series of monologues, who assaults and violates cultural forms and conventions, within the framework of a literary format that does likewise, being neither a series of short stories nor a short novel in any conventional sense. The reference to three Ubus presumably reflects Lorrain's knowledge of the fact that Jarry had written three Ubu plays, although the other two were not produced in Jarry's lifetime, or Lorrain's. Given that alliance, it is not surprising that of all Lorrain's works, *Monsieur de Bougrelon* was the one that came closest to being a precursor of surrealism, while still reflecting, in no uncertain terms, Lorrain's own particular obsessions and preoccupations. He had already established a reputation for provocation that must have allowed him to appreciate *Ubu roi* more sympathetically than the other members of the first night audience, and he continued to infuse much of his work for *Le Journal* with a sarcastic pugnacity and casual disrespect that has something in common with Alfred Jarry's rhetorical stance.

Monsieur de Bougrelon also marked a significant step forward for the employment of the regular weekly slot that Lorrain had in *Le Journal*, in which he routinely mingled fiction and non-fiction, but had previously maintained the individuality of the items. Although he had given his stories series headings before—most notably "Histoires de Masques"—the stories grouped under those headings were distinct, but *Monsieur de Bougrelon* is effectively a serial novella, appearing in weekly parts, in contrast to the daily episodes of the feuilleton serials that had been an important feature of Parisian newspapers for half a century.

Other writers for the paper, most significantly Octave Mirbeau, also grouped their short stories in series, but it was not until Lorrain had provided a key exemplar in "Contes au trois Ubus (car ils sont trois)" that some of them began developing episodic novellas and novels in a similar fashion. It was the format in which Lorrain was later to publish the novel that became his most famous and most striking work, serialized in 1899-1900 as "Astarté" and reprinted as *Monsieur de Phocas. Astarté* (1901), and it was later employed to striking effect by Edmond Haraucourt, in the serialization of *Dieudonat* (serial 1906; revised book 1912; tr. as *Dieudonat*) and *Daâh, le premier homme* (serial 1913-14; book 1914; tr. as *Daâh, the First Human*), and by Lucie Delarue-Mardrus, who serialized the majority of her novels in that fashion after 1908. Jarry and Lorrain can, therefore, be given credit for helping to prompt and promote a variant fictional format of some significance, of which *Monsieur de Bougrelon* was a key prototype.

In that context, it is worth noting that "Fleurs de banlieue" is also a variant in its format. In 1897 Lorrain was regularly mixing fictional and non-fictional contributions for his slot in *Le Journal*, writing book and theater reviews and commenting on matters of recent interest as well as supplying short stories, but it was usually easy to tell them apart. It is possible that he wrote "Fleurs de banlieue" at that time but that the editor of *Le Journal* did not run it because he thought

13

it might confuse his readers, given that it pretends to refer to items of reportage that are, in fact, pure fiction. Whether that is the case or not, the piece remains an interesting experiment in hybridization; it was not the first of its kind, and certainly not the last, but it is an intriguing oddity.

✳

"Jean Lorrain" had been born Paul-Alexandre-Martin Duval in 1855, in Fécamp, a small coastal town in Normandy, and nostalgia for his Norman childhood and ancestry features extensively in his literary works, including several items herein—although, significantly, Avranches, the particular Norman town from which Monsieur de Bougrelon and Monsieur de Mortimer hail, is located in the part of the province most distant from Fécamp. Paul's father, Amable Duval, was an apparently-prosperous but secretly profligate ship-owner whose vessels were involved in trans-Atlantic trade. After being educated at home for a while, Paul was sent to a Dominican seminary in order to complete his schooling—an experience that left him with a lifelong antipathy toward the clergy.

The Normandy shore was a favorite refuge of English exiles who crossed the channel to avoid scandal or creditors in their homeland, following a path beaten in the Georgian era by George "Beau" Brummell, whose legendary status became greater in France than in England. Algernon Swinburne, who lived near Fécamp for some years, and was once saved from drowning by Guy de

Maupassant, also a native of the region, remained the model of notoriety so far as the Duvals' home town was concerned; the lurid decor of Swinburne's house, and the scandalous things that were rumored to have gone on there, remained common knowledge long after the poet's return to England. Although Paul Duval never met Swinburne, he did become acquainted, in 1878, with Lord Arthur Somerset (1851-1926), who took vacations in the area; Somerset, who seems to have had a considerable influence on Paul's artistic tastes and attitudes, was later to cause an enormous scandal when named in an English court as a client of a male brothel in 1889.

In 1873, five years prior to meeting Somerset in the vicinity of Fécamp, Paul Duval had met Judith Gautier, the daughter of Théophile Gautier, the great pillar of the Romantic Movement, while she was on vacation there, a few months after her father's death. He was fascinated by her, although she was ten years older than him and married to, although separated from, Catulle Mendès, who was later to become one of the significant figures of the Decadent Movement. Judith Gautier does not seem to have attached any importance to Paul Duval's brief infatuation—she made no mention of it in her autobiography—but he was later to insist so ardently on the change it had wrought in his life that Edmond de Goncourt, who took him under his wing in 1885, became convinced that it had been the ruination of him. Goncourt came to believe—presumably falsely—that Lorrain's glaringly obvious but publicly-unadmitted homosexuality was a traumatic response to his doomed infatuation with Judith.

When he had completed his military service, Paul Duval was sent to Paris to study law, but he had no interest in that career, and when he announced his determination to follow a literary vocation instead, his father agreed to give him a modest allowance, on condition that the family name was veiled by a pseudonym. In 1880, therefore, Paul Duval became Jean Lorrain, and launched himself into the stereotyped lifestyle of a literary Bohemian, frequenting Le Chat Noir with the members of Émile Goudeau's literary club, the Hydropathes, and other colorful characters, including those who were to become the founders and core members of the Decadent Movement. His first collection of poetry, published under those influences, *Sang des dieux* (1882), had a frontispiece by Gustave Moreau, and Moreau's art became a considerable influence on Lorrain's literary imagery.

In 1883, before becoming a fixture at Edmond de Goncourt's weekly salon, Lorrain became a regular participant in the salon hosted by the journalist, historical novelist and Catholic polemicist Charles Buet (1846-1897), where he met the aged Jules Amédée Barbey d'Aurevilly, a proto-Decadent writer better known for his promotion of the esthetic philosophy of "dandyism," whose manifesto he had provided in *Du dandysme et de G. Brummell* (1845), and for the resultant affectations of his lifestyle. Lorrain was greatly impressed by the aged dandy, now living in much-reduced circumstances, who became his stylistic mentor, to the extent that Rémy de Gourmont was later to describe him as "the last disciple of Barbey-d'Aurevilly."

Another regular at Buet's salon, Joris-Karl Huysmans, borrowed considerable influence from Barbey-d'Aurevilly in the construction of the character of Jean Des Esseintes in his classic handbook of dandyism, *À rebours* (1884; tr. as *Against the Grain* and *Against Nature*), the book that became the prose Bible of the Decadent Movement. There is a sense in which *Monsieur de Bougrelon* is an imitative exercise, although its eponymous central character, devoid of Des Esseintes' enormous wealth, can only mimic the latter's self-indulgence in caricature and imagination, adding a further order of magnitude to his grotesquerie.

The allowance that supported Lorrain while he initially dabbled in literature was abruptly cut off when Amable Duval died in 1886, leaving nothing to his children but debts. His mother had kept control of her own money, and was not reduced to absolute penury, but she could not afford to support her son. His nascent career as a journalist became a matter of extreme urgency, but his reputation as an *enfant terrible*, already formed by his often-vitriolic reviews, was ripe for cultivation and exploitation, and he did so with great success, but not without cost. In order to maintain his ferocious rate of production, he needed recourse to artificial stimulants, and began taking ether for that purpose. The ether kept him awake, and also provided him with vivid hallucinations that he mined extensively in his short fiction, but its long-term effects on his health were catastrophic.

In 1887 Lorrain installed himself in an apartment in the Rue de Courty, which he furnished in a calculatedly bizarre fashion that took aboard the lessons he had learned from Lord Arthur Somerset, Barbey d'Aurevilly and *À rebours*. Under the hallucinogenic influence of ether, however, the apartment came to seem direly discomfiting, and he began to refer to it as his "haunted house." It was there that he wrote "La Marquise Hérode," which, although not labeled as one of his *contes d'un buveur d'éther* [ether drinker's tales], has a similar dream-like quality, and makes incidental use of an image retained from his childhood nightmares that also features in "Le Visionnaire" (1892; tr. as "The Visionary" in *Nightmares of an Ether-Drinker*). He moved to Auteuil in 1890, telling his friends that he was doing so in the hope of recovering his health and composure. He had probably given up ether-drinking by then, but if not, he certainly discontinued the habit when his mother came to live with him in 1893, although it was only in Auteuil that he began producing the definitive series of his "contes d'un buveur d'éther," which were reprinted under that subtitle in his collection *Sensations et Souvenirs* (1895).

It was in the early 1890s that the Decadent Movement and Jean Lorrain's journalistic career reached the peak of their success. Lorrain's contribution to it was quintessential, in that he became the chronicler *par excellence* of a core element of the Decadent world-view: its deliberate and insistent perversity. In particular, he focused his attention on the potential varieties of erotic perversity, producing abundant studies of erotic exoticism, particularly those characterized in Monsieur de Bougrelon as "hypothetical lusts," not only running the gamut of known fascinations and fetishisms but inventing new ones that no litterateur or psychologist had previously imagined. He detailed them in a carefully distanced, quasi-clinical fashion that scarcely masked his own intense interest, and perhaps made the author a case-study even more intriguing than the ones he invented.

There is no doubt that Lorrain's own homosexuality lies at the root of his principal literary obsession, but it is significant that homosexuality is rarely addressed directly in his stories, and when the issue does occasionally become explicit—as in such stories as "La Marquise Hérode" and "Ophélius" (1889; translated in *The Soul-Drinker and Other Decadent Fantasies*)—the attitude adopted by his narrative voices, which are invariably displaced from the characters in question, although frequently in an ambiguous relationship with them, is a horrified revulsion. More frequently, he represents characters who might seem to an objective observer to be homosexual but who are very obviously and ardently "in denial," as modern parlance puts it; Monsieur de Bougrelon is an archetypal example, in the manner in which he represents his relationship with the late Monsieur de Mortimer, and his accounts of his highly peculiar and deceptive relationships with women. Although it is always hazardous to attempt to psychoanalyze an author through his work, it is extremely difficult, on reading Jean Lorrain with a clinical eye, to avoid the inference that he was a man permanently caught between denial and self-loathing, who would dearly have liked to be at ease with himself,

19

and not to be ashamed of himself, but could not do it, in spite of all the artificial sympathy and understanding he was able to cultivate for hypothetical individuals cursed with similar problems of existence and image.

Although he was often savage in assaulting other writers in his critical essays, Lorrain seemingly reserved his most corrosive bile for homosexual writers, especially those who seemed more comfortable with their homosexuality than he was, both psychologically and socially. It was exactly a week after the first of the "contes au trois Ubus" had appeared, on 6 February, that Lorrain was called out for the most famous of the several duels occasioned by his reviews, after a scathing demolition of Marcel Proust's collection of stories and prose-poems *Les Plaisirs et les jours* (1896). The affair was settled without a shot being fired, Lorrain having presumably offered an apology that was accepted by his opponent, but the incident cannot have been without effect. It presumably contributed in some measure to the mental evolution manifest in the nine episodes presumably written thereafter—the second, "Monsieur de Mortimer," appeared the following day, on 7 February, and must already have been written.

As he had doubtless anticipated, Lorrain's days in Paris were numbered, and before the century ended he moved to the Midi, settling in Nice. He must already have embarked on "Astarté", the story series that gradually became the first of two not-quite-novels that would provide a kind of retrospective summary of the Decadent Movement and the world that had given birth to it: *Monsieur de Phocas. Astarté* and the "Coins de Byzance" section of *Le Vice errant* (1902). The former recovers several motifs from *Monsieur de Bougrelon*, although the key image of haunting eyes was not new when deployed therein. Lorrain's fortunes ran into trouble, however, when one of his former protégées, the artist Jeanne Jacquemin, recognized a portrait of herself in "Victime," a story published in *Le Journal* on 13 January 1903 (tr. as "Victim" in *Fards and Poisons*), and sued him for defamation of character. The court—presumably more desirous of expressing disapproval of the defendant than in accurately assessing the extent of any actual damage done—awarded Jacquemin absurdly high damages of eighty thousand francs, the settlement of which would have left Lorrain financially ruined had the verdict not been overturned on appeal, Jacquemin having by then relented in her pursuit, but that appeal was not heard for nine months and the precedent set by the initial verdict left him vulnerable to further attacks of the same kind; he was soon summoned to answer a formal charge of corrupting public morals by literary means, brought against *Monsieur de Phocas. Astarté*.

A legal prosecution undertaken against *Les Fleurs du mal* (1857) half a century before had called forth a loud protest and had been the making of Baudelaire's reputation, but in the case of the accusation of defamation leveled against "Victime", Lorrain found himself conspicuously lacking in support. Even his friends thought that he had overstepped the mark in his employment of Jeanne Jacquemin's tribulations as literary raw material, and there was now a considerable body of opinion in nascent twentieth-century Paris that wanted to believe and prove that the nineteenth century decadence was a thing of the past. He was, however, very disappointed that hardly anyone came forward to speak in his defense—the most notable exception was Colette—and hurt by the fact that Joris-Karl Huysmans told him privately that he thought that Jacquemin was justified.

Lorrain continued to write at a furious pace in 1903 in order to pay his legal expenses, but what he produced gradually lost impetus, and much of the work he published in and after 1904 gave the impression of being hackwork, lacking the distinction of his earlier material. The new projects that he started in 1903 mostly ran out of steam fairly quickly. The two story series launched in *Le Journal* in June 1903 that are translated herein are both examples of the latter tendency, although they are interesting exercises, the first group of four stories making a deliberate nostalgic return to the Normandy of his childhood and to the fascination with tales of the marvelous that he had at the time, overlaid by a newly-sharpened cynical disenchantment. It is not surprising that the two tales set in Provence are uneasy in their ambiance, in spite of the fact that the author was now permanently resident in the Midi, and although they contain scathing character studies of the kind that had become his standard literary strategy, their cutting edge is a trifle chipped and blunted, even by comparison with "La Femme au tigre," written only a year earlier, but—crucially—before "Victime" and its fall-out.

Lorrain's health continued to deteriorate after 1903, but he went on working stubbornly and ardently. In June 1906, although he can hardly have been fit to travel, he returned to Paris to assist in the preparations for the production of an opera based on the most famous of his many fabular *contes*, "La Princess sous verre" (1896; tr. as "The Princess Under Glass") and to obtain further treatment from Pozzi; he died there of peritonitis when one of the ulcers in his colon perforated explosively while he was attempting to self-administer an enema. He left a literary legacy that was as varied as it is controversial, and it has retained its controversial quality even into the twenty-first century, when there has been something of a renaissance of interest in his work.

Although there is a definite artificiality about the provocative quality of Lorrain's work, which strives hard for its effects—too hard, on occasion—it is not dishonest. His character studies are caricaturish, and Monsieur de Bougrelon is one of the most caricaturish of all, although the company he keeps here illustrates the extent to which he was also typical of the author's narrative method and theories of human nature, but he is not simply a cartoon figure; he has a real substance, and the narrator's fascination with him is perfectly understandable; he really does have a heroic dimension, just as his author, while writing copiously, and sometimes desperately, in order to make a living, also had a heroic dimension in his explorations of literary effect, and in his enduring assault on human pretention and hypocrisy. He never feigned innocence of the faults that he was analyzing and parodying, always aware that his expertise in depicting characters possessed of a monstrous dimension was based on aspects of his own character that were certainly not beyond reproach, but nevertheless deserving of respect, and even of awe.

Although *Monsieur de Phocas. Astarté* is a portmanteau work, akin in that regard to *Monsieur de Bougrelon*, its greater substance and continuity allowed it to pass more easily for a novel, and because it is not quite as provocative a work, or as unorthodox, it has always reaped the greater applause; it is nowadays regarded as Lorrain's masterpiece. *Monsieur de Bougrelon* is considerably more idiosyncratic, more akin to the phantom of a novel than a substantial work of fiction, just as its hero is more akin to the phantom of a dandy than a coherent individual, but that makes it more interesting in some ways, and it is certainly a work of considerable importance, which benefits from being read in concert with *Monsieur de Phocas* and other studies of a similar kind, especially the one nested within *Le Vice errant*.

Bizarre as he is, it is surely possible for a modern reader to feel more sympathy for the ill-fated Monsieur de Bougrelon than for the splenetic aristocrat who eventually transforms himself into "Monsieur de Phocas," or for the horrid bearer of a strange family curse in "Coins de Byzance." For all its calculated eccentricity, *Monsieur de Bougrelon* is a strangely poignant work, and it is not surprising that its central character continued to haunt the author long after he had concluded the series of vignettes composing the work. As literary revenants go, he is one of those most likely to make a liminal but profound impression even in today's world.

✳

24

The translation of *Monsieur de Bougrelon* was made from the version of the text reproduced in the 1999 Robert Laffont Bouquins anthology *Romans fin-de-siècle*, the Lotus Bleu version reproduced on *archive.org* being rather difficult to read, as are the eleven items in the issues of *Le Journal* reproduced on *gallica*. The translations of stories from *Du temps que les bêtes parlaient* were made from the copy of the Courrier français edition reproduced on *gallica*, although the original versions of "La Femme au tigre" and "La Marquise Hérode" were also consulted in the copies of periodicals reproduced on *gallica*.

MONSIEUR DE BOUGRELON

AND OTHER STORIES

MONSIEUR DE BOUGRELON

I
The Café Manchester

AMSTERDAM is always water, and houses painted in black and white, all windows, with sculpted gables and guipure curtains: black and white redoubled in the water. Thus, it is always the water, the dead water, the shimmering water and the gray water, pathways of water that never end, canals guarded by lodgings like enormous games of dominoes. That could be funereal, and yet it is not sad; it is, however, a trifle monotonous at length, especially when it is frosty and the fixed tinplate of the canals no longer mirrors the lovely little doll's-houses with their doorsteps in the air and heads down.

Thus, there was a strong wind that day on the Amstel, a wind to sweep away the road-sweepers themselves; on the Dam, there was the spectacle, already seen too many times, of the tram-station and the crowd around it: fur hats pulled down over violet-tinged ears, conductors and coachmen florid with acne burrowing into scarves;

and those strange little old men who, with an eternal drop of ice at the tip of a red nose, sell you omnibus tickets more dearly than at the office—but everyone must live, and the astonishment of hearing "dangyew" instead of *merci*, and receiving their shivering mucus on the back of one's glove, is one of the pleasures of tourism in Holland . . .

Oh, those people of the North! Anyway, Holland is rather ugly, and the Dutch resemble it; the old ladies with black velvet hats over lace bonnets ornamented at the temples with perforated gold plates, evidently suit old master paintings better than the ambiance of the streets; the Seadeck[1]—the Rydeck of Amsterdam—only comes to life at night. As for the Ness, where worthy and buxom fellows, blond, pink and plump with expansive faces, hang about innocently on the threshold of taverns, crammed into long overcoats like those of hotel porters, it has no mystery for us; we have already visited it too frequently—and that is human ingratitude, because did not the Ness delight us sufficiently on the first evening?

Have we appreciated sufficiently those heavy doors opening abruptly to allow the appearance behind a row of tables of a heap of chairs and bales of straw, stood like a dessert on a distant and luminous stage. "French ladies, come in, Messieurs, French is spoken"—and that on the part of chubby-faced giants, with rever-

---

1 Lorrain appears to have invented this name, and also "le Ness," although the latter is presumably a variant of "le Nes," which appears as a district of Amsterdam in some earlier French texts, including *Abraham Pinedo, docteur d'Amsterdam* (1833) by Arnold da Costa, and there is indeed a Rue des Nes in the city.

ences and thick-lipped smiles, but good, honest smiles nonetheless, smiles unknown in Paris. They do not let go for a minute of the cordon they hold in their hand; and there is along that Rue des Ness, on every threshold, the same sudden appearance of nudities and flamboyant fabrics, the same patriotic offer—*French ladies*—and the same greeting.

Oh, how many French ladies there are in all the Nesses of foggy Belgiums, distant Hollands and all lands!

> *Oh how proud one is of being French*
> *When one travels abroad.*

It is restful and refreshes the soul, that ardent quarter of Amsterdam; a *bonhomie* reigns there unknown in the Latin countries, and those brave showmen of the Inferno, those solid porters of the devil, disarm malevolence with their benevolent varnished faces, their huge fur-gloved hands, and their appearance of honest butlers beneath their gold-braided caps. Evidently, though, we have seen too much of them.

Ness, Seadeck, the Dam and even the Museum have no more to say to us. There are days like that in life; we wandered through the city along the frozen canals, like wrecks, hastening our steps at the street corners because of the strong wind—because, as I have already said, it was blowing mightily that day in the Amstel.

It was cold enough to freeze a duck, and a wild duck at that, and the numerous schiedams we had downed in all the cellars of Calverstraat had scarcely cheered us up—there are days like that in life—and we were ambling along in the January wind, woeful and miserable, when a singular sign startled us:

CAFÉ MANCHESTER

It was, in one of those uniformly black and white streets of Amsterdam, a little old two-story dwelling, but very low beneath an enormous roof that coiffed it from the gable almost to the ground floor. It seemed gathered in on itself, as if going underground, because it was necessary to go down five steps to find the door and the only real window, a large display-window completely fitted with a lace curtain, opening almost at ground level; on the other floors there were irregular little loopholes with closed shutters: *Café Manchester.* The dwelling had an antiquated appearance; it even had a pulley at the top of its roof in order to haul up food supplies and furniture. What did they sell in that café—in the Café Manchester, where French and English were evidently spoken?

The cold was bitter, the house equivocal; we went in.

"Come in, Messieurs, sit down, these ladies will come: Deborah, eh! Gudule, here are French messieurs."

That was a very venerable old lady, with a huge black velvet hood posed on a lace bonnet: an old lady with a shawl, bracelets and cameos, and in the little low room there was a minuet step, a toothy smile and, knees bent, three plunging bows. They are much less correct in France: what posture, what reserve and what distinction!

We had taken our places; oh, what a familial interior, the table polished and shiny, the furniture waxed like mirrors, the walls washed and lustrous, like moiré silk, with reflections everywhere, and a nice faience stove at the back. There was even a hardwood pipe-rack, with pipes—the pipes that Jan Peters and Cornelis must have smoked in the evenings.

It was charming, but the demoiselles were less so.

Low in the backside and short-legged, an oakum blonde with an absent profile and a rather heightened complexion, Deborah was familiar, even enterprising. Playful by temperament, she might have been pleasing at eighteen, but the Café Manchester had evidently crumpled her and thickened her, and the poor girl, as red as roast beef and as fleecy as a sheep, put a deplorable insistence into climbing on to our knees and sipping from our glasses. Her cheeks, sandpapered like the copper of tankards, had a fulgurant gleam.

Deborah was clean and well-rinsed, an interior of her homeland, but she had rather sparse hair, insipid blue eyes and soft flesh emitting a perfume of heady musk; in addition, an affectionate, even caressant nature, with hands easily led astray and a touching obsession for repeating: "Relax, Monsieur, *take it easy*."

Gudule was even less alluring. Hailed by the mistress of the abode at the moment when she was struggling to scrub the floor of one of the upstairs rooms, that fine ancillary—a real workhorse—had run downstairs in the summary attire of a worthy skivvy: a cotton camisole thrown over a skirt, and bare feet in clogs. An

"At your service, Monsieur!" time to make an abrupt bow, "You'll buy me a beer, won't you?" and Gudule was installed.

If Deborah reeked of musk, Gudule stank of warm water and potash; her breasts were firm but the flesh of her arms was grainy and pock-marked like that of a turkey—the arms of a washerwoman, good for pleasing carters. Beneath her sleeves, boldly rolled up, there was a gossip, who did not turn up her nose at a glass of beer or male kisses; a true Teniers,[1] square-framed and hard-limbed; but the face was rather ugly and her smile had a few holes; the humidity of the Netherlands is so deadly to delicate dentition.

Deborah had lit a lamp; the lady in the black hat, seated to one side, had stuck an enormous pair of spectacles on her nose, and was rapidly plying long, slender needles, bent over her knitting. From time to time she hazarded a discreet glance in our direction, and a benevolent smile, a mute: *go on, my lads, don't hold back* that reassured and softened the atmosphere of quietude and tranquility; we had already offered five schiedams to Deborah and four bottles of beer to Gudule. Oh, that peaceful and familial Dutch interior!

It was at that moment that he appeared.

He, *him*: the epic silhouette of that land of fog, that city of dreams, the prestigious hero of these tales: he

---

1 The reference is to the work of the painter David Teniers the younger (1610-1690), the most famous and most prolific member of a family of artists.

opened the door very wide, with a single thrust, and stood on the threshold, waiting.

What an entrance! The man who presents himself thus surely has genius. Belted at the waist in a long tubular frock-coat, his shoulders broad and his torso thin, an enormous top hat tilted to one side, a brawler, he was, with the frightful cudgel he was holding in his hand, a figure already seen elsewhere and all the more unforgettable for it. The figure of a policeman, an old stager or a half-pay officer, he was simultaneously Javert, the retreat from Russia and Frederick Lemaître.[1]

The frock-coat was green, and what a threadbare green! The gaiter-strapped trousers were twisted like a corkscrew over fine cambered and polished boots, but gaping at the heel. His red woolen muffler, very long around the neck, was a much-darned rag, ragged and holed; but as such, with his old captain's face painted and plastered, his bloodshot and charcoal-blacked eyes, with his toothless mouth beneath a waxed moustache, that ragamuffin was a great lord, that marionette personified a race, that clown was a soul.

The two girls had got up. Still camped in the frame of the door, where his silhouette was further magnified, the man had folded his arms, and, his cudgel tightly clutched against his breast now, he leaned backwards and smiled.

"Well, my kittens," he growled, in a cavernous voice, "aren't you going to enjoy my treats today? I

_____

1 Inspector Javert is Jean Valjean's nemesis in Victor Hugo's *Les Misérables*; Frederick Lemaître was a famous actor whose athletic build equipped him admirably for playing lusty parts.

have sweets for you, though; I know how greedy you are, usually."

And, with a gesture of the ancient court, having spread a few grains of tobacco on the back of his hand, he replaced an ignoble whitewood box in his fob pocket, and, with a sniff of his broad nostrils, sucked it up with a single breath.

"Real Spanish tobacco, which a friend, the Marquis de Las Marimas Tolosas, sends me every year from Havana, on which you're fasting today, Mesdemoiselles, for I find you ingrate. The old friend has been forgotten. Lovers of passage are toying with you, my doves, and if these Messieurs weren't French—oh, if you weren't French, Messieurs, I warn you—there would be an affair, yes, Messieurs, an affair to settle tomorrow outside the city bounds; but I'm too glad to greet my compatriots here.

"These little madcaps wouldn't be making so much fuss over you if you had been Dutch. They're gallant, and hold out for Paris. I'm from the Île-de-France, Messieurs, more Parisian than Madame de Staël, who was born in the Rue du Bac; I'm from the suburbs—the suburbs, that girdle of foam of flowers of Paris—and a charming corner, in verity, that of Bas-Meudon, Messieurs; the water-bus stops three times a day at the bottom of the terrace of my forefathers' château. The Black Band destroyed it, alas."[1]

And, very noble, having uncovered his bald head—only bald for a moment, because the wig carried away

---

1 The Black Band were German mercenaries who fought in the French army in the sixteenth century

by the hat fell back on to the cranium: "My name is Monsieur de Bougrelon, Messieurs."[1]

＊

"Gin, Deborah, and my own gin." And when the girl had placed before the old eccentric a bottle of Delft as large and bulbous as a goat's udder, in its wicker basket: "I never drink anything but the eighteen-fifty; these drugs need forty years in the bottle; returned from India, these Northern alcohols are sometimes marvelous, but I owe you the truth; this one hadn't sailed; it's in good taste, however. May I offer you some, Messieurs?"

He spoke with his head held high, in a declamatory and lofty tone of a noble father, his stomach protruding like a prow, his shoulders thrust back in an exaggerated fashion. Deborah had filled our glasses and, catching her in passage, he had sat her down on his knee: an extravagant and almost tragic group, that slattern astride the meager thighs of that ancestor with the spectral head: a swaggering and lecherous specter, for he had slid one hand under the girl's shirts and with the other—the desiccated hand of a mummy, evidently very fine once, but macabre beneath the heavy rings

_____

1 The first of the eleven episodes in *Le Journal* ends here; the character introduces himself in that version as "Monsieur de Baugrelon" but that is presumably a misprint. Between the first and second episodes, however, the physical description of the character alters somewhat. The fact that his Parisian origin vanishes is less surprising, as the accounts he gives of himself contain numerous inconsistencies. The second episode in *Le Journal* was entitled "Monsieur de Mortimer."

of gilded copper passed over all the fingers—he was smoothing his stiff, dyed moustache.

It was almost a scene from Holbein, in the iridescent half-light of that dive: that fat slut, too pink in the flesh and too blonde, rubbing herself seductively against that painted, corseted, powdered and cravated cadaver, beneath his red muffler, like a Regency roué, in a flood of gold lace: Prostitution pampering Death.

But Monsieur de Bougrelon was not disarmed. "You're newly disembarked in Amsterdam, Messieurs? Is it indiscreet to ask since when? You've already roamed the city, visited the museums, the churches and the whores. Amsterdam is, *palsambleu*, a rather mysterious city; its houses seem transparent, open to all comers; there's nothing but windows, or at least one might think so, and we fops—we all are, in France—think we possess the city, the Dutch and the Netherlands, Rotterdam and The Hague, even the Zuiderzee, the entire North Sea, in three turns. Error, Messieurs: Holland is a coquette, she offers everything and gives nothing; the water in the canals is very deep; the boats are reflected there and don't sink; if they sank, Messieurs, they'd never be seen again. Amsterdam, Rotterdam and all the Dams in the world are built over gulfs, on piles—remember that.

"It's through those piles that I want to pilot you, Messieurs. Your insouciant ignorance charms me and moves me to compassion; one is not entirely a fop. In truth, it's delightful: the houses of this land appear to you to be glass, but they're horn, Messieurs; cuckoldry flourishes there like tulips, but rejects all foreign stuffing. There's nothing but windows, you've said, but there are no doors, or so few: doll's houses, but all the more dangerous for it because the doll is a woman, a woman dolled up and made up, all futility and lies, because she's empty and has no soul; and it's that void that attracts us, we men; it's the gulf, the eternal gulf of cities with Dams, on piles."

Suddenly interrupting his lecture to sniff Deborah's camisole at close range, he said: "Your flesh is fine enough, my girl, but your musk is poisonous. Where did you get that perfume? The barber who sold it to you was surely a cook; it's goose-grease that you've put on! Tomorrow I'll send you a flask of bergamot and a pot of almond paste prepared with amaryllis juice."

And, having stood up abruptly, just taking time to remove the grains of tobacco stick between his gold teeth with a toothpick, Monsieur de Bougrelon negligently picked up his cane, leaving us to settle the bill.

"Amsterdam awaits; permit me, Messieurs, to do the honors for you." And as the two whores followed us to the door, soliciting: "A little modesty, Mesdemoiselles; do you take us for sailors? Can't you see that these Messieurs are gentlemen? We'll come back."

Flemish gibberish greeted that promise—surely insults. Our exit was jeered. In fact, something extraordinary happened. Gudule, whom I thought meeker, furious at seeing that her clients were being taken away, seized Monsieur de Bougrelon around the waist, his thin and belted waist, and, lifting him off the ground in her robust arms, caused him to pirouette in mid-air like a wisp of straw, and then deposited him on the ground; and there was a loud, insulting laughter at the old man's weakness.

"She's a little familiar," Monsieur de Bougrelon contented himself with saying. "It's stifling in this dive, Messieurs."

After having walked for some time together, as we emerged on to a street on the bank of a canal, our strange companion interjected:

"A fine spectacle, geometrical and calm, one of the few that suit tumultuous souls. It's almost thirty years, Messieurs, that I've been living in the Netherlands; the adventure that brought me here is a very sad story, and, as you've guessed, a love story. Yes, it was some thirty years ago that I left France. We settled initially in The Hague, Monsieur de Mortimer and I—for I exiled myself for a man, Messieurs; although, naturally, there was a woman at the bottom of it. In eighteen forty we still had those heroic amities.[1] When Mortimer was obliged to leave Avranches after his duel with Lord Finghal, I went with him, Messieurs. Could I have allowed a friend of twenty years to go away, far from his family and his hearth, alone? A man with whom all my mistresses were smitten, and who, in more than two hundred assaults, disarmed me at the third pass, and without taking any vanity therefrom, Messieurs?

"For twenty years and more we had had the same women and the same horses, and when, in that unfortunate duel with Lord Finghal, the honesty of Monsieur de Mortimer was suspected . . .

---

1 The chronology of this passage makes no sense, but that is typical of the character—although the failure of the narrative voice to comment on it might seem a trifle odd.

"That great terrible child had aroused frightful resentments in the little town of Avranches; he was strangely handsome, and that is the one thing that a man will not pardon another man, Messieurs. He was proud too, with a charming pride that enraged all the fops in the province; do you imagine that that adored man never breathed a word about his successes? Given that, how could he not have had enemies?

"So, we emigrated together. Paris, where the gross Orléans ruled, was too small for us, and it was The Hague that lodged us first; yes, The Hague had that honor, The Hague and its royal museum, where so many handsome portraits often appeared to us as our own resemblance, for I too was handsome in my fashion. We turned a few heads there in that aristocratic and tranquil Hague; the frame there was at the level of our persons, and on the evenings of balls at Court, the 'Another unfortunate coming for me,' with which Mortimer welcomed the entrance of every woman was not such a bold paradox as might have been thought. Who could have resisted his prestigious elegance, that profile of a young god—but a god of Versailles, as majestic as a Bourbon and impertinent as a Lauzun,[1] a regal god and a great lord?

"He had brought from our royalist Normandy refinements of dress and an expertise of style that were

---

1 Antoine Nompar de Caumont, Duc de Lauzun (1632-1793) was one of the most influential figures at the court of Louis XIV, although his turbulent nature often landed him in trouble and he was imprisoned several times. His reputation was given a further twist in the nineteenth century when Barbey d'Aurevilly, in his book on dandyism, nominated him as an archetypal dandy *avant la lettre*.

bound to subjugate those barbaric Zeelanders. Oh, if you had seen him take his turn around the park between two and four, in the foggy days of winter, or saluting the beautiful ladies amid the quincunxes, around the fishpond, on frosty mornings, coming out of mass at the château. There were palatines[1] of sable at fifty louis the skin, Messieurs; houppleandes of episcopal violet woolen cloth lined with blue fox-fur; enormous muffs, true sapper's bonnets in the fur of spaniels as blonde as women's hair and which, in order to salute the infantas, he removed with a hand gloved in otter-skin. Extraordinary gloves, Messieurs, each finger of which had nails of agate—a tiger's paw or the devil's hand—an invention of his own, of an entirely delightful eccentricity, which was typical of him.

"He was the one who launched, first of all, the black velvet hat with a large buckle of Cape diamonds over a moiré silk ribbon; and in the evening, when he went into society, he powdered his moustache, which was blond and very handsome, with a strange mixture of blue and gold powder. From a distance, one might have sworn that it was a scarab, an Egyptian scarab, posed on a pink rose, for, until the very last day, he had the most vermilion lips, which might have been thought to be painted with the blood of hearts.

"How could one resist such fantasies?

---

1 A palatine was a fur tippet or stole, made fashionable at Louis XIV's court by the Princess Palatine. I shall leave the many other references to obsolete items of clothing undefined, the nature of most of them being deducible from context.

"And that hero had to go into exile because of the wife of a petty magistrate at the court of Caen—for Mortimer was a Norman like me, Messieurs. We were both of that race of giants, blond and strong, bold in conquest and bold in amour, imperishable adventurers whose blue blood still flourishes in the meadows of London, an immortal race whose irrepressible spirit of adventure had conquered India and all its colonies for England.

"It, was, therefore, for the wife of that petty magistrate, of the tawdry *noblesse de robe* and insignificant in beauty, believe me, that Mortimer picked a quarrel with Lord Finghal, a colonel in the third Highland Regiment, then on leave in our old city of Caen, for our fat and warm Normandy then attracted a good many of those tall English wading-birds in winter. In brief, for a trifle, Madame de Bresveville being looked at too closely; my friend, who was courting the little quail, provoked the impertinent and, at twenty paces, in a pathway in the park, fractured the skull of that English ogler of women, but in a singular fashion that put the authorities on our heels. A freak of chance, in truth, a most unexpected fatality, which determined that Lord Finghal was killed by his own bullet . . .

"Monsieur de Mortimer had a skull so hard—of granite, Messieurs—that the accursed Englishman's bullet ricocheted from his forehead and killed our fine Highlander stone dead. He fell like a dead weight at the end of our path, his head shattered. Mortimer couldn't get over it. 'I repel bullets,' he contented himself with saying as he handed me his weapon. But that evening we had to quit the town with all possible haste.

"Were we not accused of murder? Yes, Monsieurs, it was put forward that I, Mortimer's witness, had fired at and killed my friend's adversary. We would not have been accused of that if they knew us, to be sure! An infamous machination, Monsieur, and well worthy of a town in which country lawyers whose ancestors served at table sit in the tribunal!

"We decamped at dusk, persuaded but not convinced by the Marquise de Brindecourt, who lent us her berline. We could not resist that white-haired noble lady's tears. Mortimer venerated her after the fashion of his mother, whom he had never seen; the dowager had raised him on her knees; that great heart could not bear to see the august kneecaps on which he had played as a child dragging themselves over the floor-tiles . . .

"We left, Messieurs, on the saddest rainy evening, so sad that one might have thought that the entire sky of Normandy was weeping. We never saw that land again, and it is thus that that hero, the last descendant of a race of gallant knights, which ought never to have become extinct, spoiled the most beautiful future— and all for a little woman with oakum-blonde hair, at whom you would not have glanced in Paris. But that's life. A pebble on the road can make a giant stumble.

"But a rendezvous obliges me to leave you, Messieurs; I had not foreseen the pleasure of encountering you. A woman of the nobility, who wishes me well, is waiting for me; besides, you ought to be at home in Calverstraat;

I am at your disposal tomorrow, provided that I am not importunate, Messieurs. Your hotel? I can be there at nine o'clock, under arms, only too glad if I can enable you to see some corners of Amsterdam worthy of your curiosity."

A great sweep of the hat, a sudden straightening of his upper body, and he had disappeared.

II
The Tattooed Spaniard[1]

"The Museum! It's to the Museum that I'm taking you!"

At nine o'clock precisely, as he had said the day before, Monsieur de Bougrelon was at our hotel. His legs a trifle stiff, but with a majestic stride, he was pacing back and forth in the hall, his upper body drawn up even more impertinently than usual, to the great scandal of the worthy Dutchmen around the tables, scoffing mortadella, sausages and immense cups of café au lait.

Alerted by the porter, who had come up to our rooms to inform us that a fairground performer was asking for us down below, we had immediately divined who he meant. A fairground performer! That old Norman gentleman, that son of the ancient pirates, conquerors of the three isles! Decidedly, abroad as in

---

1 In the series in *Le Journal*, this episode is entitled "Les Patenôtres de rubis" [The Rosary of Rubies].

45

France, the servant class everywhere has the same crass irreverence for everything that is heroic poverty and ragged grandiloquence.

We went downstairs in all haste, in order to avoid an insult to the last representative of an illustrious race. We were just in time; the entire staff of the hotel, as well as people staying at the Adrian, valets and waiters, had formed a circle around Monsieur de Mortimer's prestigious friend. Also, that morning, Monsieur de Bougrelon had truly gone over the top.

In our honor, the old beau had put on a Carmelite cloth houppelande and a fur bonnet that took our breath away. With brandenburgs of olive silk and the brightly illuminated braid of a Magyar dolman, tightened at the waist and hanging down to the knees, it was a garment unexpected even in Amsterdam, where pedestrians in the street still wear the costume of Admiral Ruyter.[1] It was everything that one could wish, except a houppelande: the dressing-gown of Argan,[2] the kaftan of a Caucasian chief, the pelisse of a Polish Jew—something extravagant and unnamable, and yet already seen in the retreat from Russia, an epic garment that would have made the fortune of a leading dramatic role on a boulevard stage.

An old otter-skin hat, as large as a sombrero, coiffed that spectral old head like a diadem. Russian leather boots, on which silver spurs rotated in enormous row-

---

1 Michiel de Ruyter (1607-1676), famous for his role in the Anglo-Dutch Wars

2 Argan is the protagonist of Molière's *Le Malade Imaginaire*, who wore a dressing-gown in bed, as befits a hypochondriac.

els, completed the accoutrement. Finally, over his two hands, the old marionette wore, pressed against his breast, a fabulous muff, once black and now russet, a muff that was curly, frayed and eroded, evidently the hide of some old lap-dog.

And he smiled, the monster, and said in a peremptory tone: "I've gone to some trouble. How do you like me?" And, pirouetting on the spot: "Do your Parisian tailors know nowadays how to cut such a houppelande in their Elbeuf cloth? Feel the grain of this fabric, and see how it grips my waist without pinching my hips! What liberty in the shoulders. I'm at home in it. And this hat is virgin otter, Messieurs. When I put it on for the first time it was at the on the pond at Groningen, skating in the park. Duchess Wilhelmine—an exquisite woman, whose like no longer exists—was giving a nocturnal fête there, with costumes, sleighs, torches and masks. It was one of the last enchantments of the century.[1] The duchess appeared there as a Mongol princess and I was a Greenlander lord; we were never apart that night. The *Gazette de la Haye* talked for an entire week about that Mongolian Princess and that Duke of Greenland! Monsieur de Mortimer was dressed in the fabulous costume of a Sultan of Samarkand. *Tudieu!* We knew how to spend money, we exiles!

"So, I got this hat for that ball; I say ball, but it was for skating, and above all for banter, but amorous ban-

1 The reference is fictitious, and cannot denote Wilhelmine of Prussia (1774-1837), who became Queen of the Netherlands by marriage, although the author evidently has someone akin to her in mind.

47

ter, elegant, affected, frivolous and passionate, futile and somber. For one sometimes dies, yes, for an exchanged glance, or a grip of the hand in the shadows—what do I know?—a surprised kiss . . . yes, we were like that. I got this hat for that exquisite fête and that even more exquisite woman; a few gold tassels decorated it, with a pearl furbelow. The furbelow is strung out as a nostalgic border around a painting on ivory that you'll see in my home when you have the honor of crossing my threshold, Messieurs. The gold tassels I removed, like those on my boots; it is necessary to be able to make sacrifices to the prejudices of our epoch; above all, it is necessary sometimes to resign oneself to the preconceived ideas of our dear friends, isn't it, Messieurs?"

And, with a thin smile: "Believe, Messieurs, that if I still had my income of a hundred thousand livres, my elegance would be more discreet, but poverty owes it to itself to be ostentatious; only millionaires have the right to garments the color of soot." And with a brisk pirouette of that long arthritic body: "It's to the Museum, Messieurs, that I'm taking you."

And when we were in the street, he said to us, in a melancholy tone: "I always draw a little crowd here. Behind the times as this region is, it has made progress, and I've remained stationary. I'm an idea, in an era when there no longer are any. Although newcomers in Amsterdam, you seem to them to fit in, while I, who have lived among them for forty years, I . . . but the strange is foreign everywhere. Fidelity is so eccentric— what am I saying? It's worse than eccentric; it's an exile, Messieurs. Who is faithful, today? And the exile is always alone.

"Now, that solitude is my pride. I'm in the pillory, but I'm looking down at the crowd. What can it matter to me, who has known a sublime friendship, who has lived in the company of ideal women—the last women, understand me, Messieurs, of a society that has disappeared forever—what, I ask you, can the little cries of fright of bourgeois at windows, and street-urchins turning their backs on me, or the gibes of passers-by at the religion of the past, matter to me? People mock me, and I congratulate myself for it, yes, I congratulate myself, Messieurs. Better than that, Messieurs: I'm crazy for it."

And as we acquiesced, with a smile, to the sadness, touching, in sum, of his braggadocio: "Do you like Museums, Messieurs? Monsieur de Mortimer and I spent the best hours of our exile there. Oh, the portraits of women! The long enchantments poured out by the painted gazes of those portraits! I don't know if you sense, as I do, Messieurs, that there is magic in certain faces of the old masters. Such as you see me, when I lived in Florence—for I've lived in Italy—I spent two hours every morning in the Uffizi. I had three mistresses there, three dead women of whom the living would have been jealous, and rightly so; and indeed, of all the living ones I've known, with only one exception, time has made ashes and tears, while those three portraits . . .

"One was by Leonardo—as you'll have guessed, a man like me always likes da Vinci—another by Bernardino Luini; it represented a courtesan, a red-haired woman, but a red that only those Italians knew how to paint, with rubies and pearls woven into her

49

golden tresses. I say a courtesan, but surely a Herodias,[1] for she was carrying—with what style!—a bloody head on a silver platter, and hideous as that head was, with a serous pallor and revulsed irises, I would have liked that head to be mine, and I would have consented to being beheaded in order to be triumphantly carried by that triumphant woman. That Herodias had arched eyebrows and an arched mouth, eyebrows so black and a mouth so royally made up, that the thunderbolt was triple. Oh, those three taut bows! Cupid was lying in ambush behind each of them, and there was a triple release and a triple strike too, first in the head, then straight in the heart, and the last . . . you know where.

"The terrible woman, terrible and exquisite—but that one, I had a reason to love. She was the indecent and perilous resemblance of an adorable and wild Spaniard. I say Spaniard and I see you smile. Although I had known her in Paris, that Spaniard was from a great family, Messieurs; she was born Dela Morozina Campéador Cantès, and she was a heroic woman. Married at thirteen to a Mexican general killed during the insurrection, she had witnessed the taking of Puebla; better than that, she had defended it.[2]

1 French writers occasionally regarded the names of Herodias and Salome as interchangeable; the description is of Luini's *Salome with the Head of John the Baptist*, now in the Boston Museum of Fine Arts, but Lorrain might have confused that painting in his memory with Luini's *Erodiade* [Herodias] in the Uffizi, which he must also have seen.
2 The city of Puebla was in the heart of the region most afflicted during the Mexican War of Independence. Its name would have been most familiar to Lorrain's contemporary readers as the location of a significant battle during the French intervention in Mexico, in 1862.

"She had a portrait of her husband tattooed on her left breast, and when she bared it for a ball, that glimpsed tattoo resembled a network of lace, a fragment of a mantilla on the white of her skin; it was divine, an exquisite refinement of coquetry, an epic tattoo that made her more beautiful. One might have liked to efface the image of her husband from her bosom by the force of kisses, but it was indelible; the Marquise Della Morozina Campéador Cantès was inaccessible.

"During the capture of Puebla she had been subjected to the horrors of rape—an atrocious rape, Messieurs; twenty chiefs of the insurgents had disputed with pistol shots the savage voluptuousness of possessing her first; they discharged two hundred bullets. Five of those fanatics perished, and the unfortunate woman suffered the violation of the other fifteen, fuming with lust and carnage, while laid on the five cadavers still warm.

"She did not die of it, Messieurs, but she made a vow of chastity.

"A truly womanly woman who has known the horrible sensuality of fifteen rapes is defended by the memory; the Marquise was one of those. Hers was a soul matured in terror, a flesh congealed in indignation.

"And yet, what coquetry! She had brought back from Mexico the most beautiful jewels; but, an implausible cachet, she only ever wore rubies, bloody stones on a woman once bloodied; she wore them like a cilice; it was there that the passionate savagery of her soul burst forth. She wore rubies without mounts, fifteen rubies—for there were fifteen, in memory of her fifteen

51

rapists—and those attestatory rubies she had had embedded in her skin.

"They were fifteen drops of blood that pearled translucently on the nudity of her flesh, fifteen brilliant gems on her shoulders, perforated by fifteen wounds, fifteen scars that reopened every time she went to a ball, Messieurs, for although she was too coquettish to renounce society entirely, she tortured her body in expiation, her adornment became a torment for her. It would have been necessary, Messieurs, admit it, to be a terrible fop to dare to talk of amour to a woman who wore, bleeding, round her neck, the memory of fifteen rapes, with a portrait of her husband on her left breast—and what a portrait, Messieurs: tattooed, as I've said.

"That terrible conceit, that inconceivable and childish audacity, someone nevertheless had one evening, and that someone was not Monsieur de Mortimer, and it was not Monsieur de Lafraité-Junance, the most handsome officer in the king's guard, it was . . . but here we are at the Museum, Messieurs; we have arrived."

And with a childish gaucherie: "I told you, Messieurs, that I adored Luini's Herodias with a savage amour because of a resemblance; I have, therefore. compromised the Marquise . . . which would be dastardly if that exquisite woman had had the slightest weakness for me. The Marquise Della Morozina Campéador Cantès"—Monsieur de Bougrelon took off his hat— "died twenty years ago, having retired to Avranches, to a little house that still belonged to me two years ago. I've sold it since, and that was one of the great chagrins of my life.

"Ruined by bankers, the Marquise Della Morozina Campéador Cantès consented to accept, for eight years of her life, the modest pension I was able to provide for her; she consented because she could, never having been my mistress." Monsieur de Bougrelon was still speaking with his hat in his hand. "A Marquise Della Morozina cannot be kept like a whore, but a gallant man may aid a friend: that was the way we were once, in Avranches.

"Mercedes—for her name was Mercedes—thought about me, however, in her last hour; the rosary on which I say my *paternosters*, you will see in my home beneath her miniature: my rosary, Messieurs, each of whose *paters* is composed of three large rubies.[1]

> *Of the long enchantments poured forth by*
> *the gazes*
> *Of old portraits of women displayed in the*
> *Louvre*
> *More than one man bears a weeping open*
> *wound in the side,*
> *That gives him a blanched face, and hag-*
> *gard gestures.*

"That wound in the side, Messieurs, I have borne all my life, for, all my life, I have had a sad and foolish love of old portraits. Those verses, written in my youth—for I too have been a poet, like everyone else—still summarizes the bewildered nostalgia of my soul, that nostalgic and haughty soul, which made me, between the ages of

---

1 The episode in *Le Journal* ends here; the next bears the title "Nostalgiques poupées" [Nostalgic Dolls]

eighteen and twenty-five, the ecstasized and assiduous devotee of the museums of Dresden and Italy.

"Monsieur de Mortimer also had that soul. Our friendship, Messieurs, was a eucharist; we took communion in the same admirations, and loved in the same hatreds. It was at the altar of masters that we were seen kneeling, but we stood up in the oratory of beautiful women: inclined before Art, we were upstanding before Beauty. Oh, the smiles of da Vinci, Messieurs, what a poem of perverse and regal ferocity, the kisses of leeches in which our souls were engulfed.

"Personally, the *Mona Lisa* sucked me in completely. And Botticelli's women likewise, the grace of their fugitive and gracile nudity, the spice of their thinness, especially the *Primavera*![1] Such as you see me, Messieurs, I was infatuated for two years with that nymph with the face of a ghoul—for she is a ghoul, and perhaps worse. The ambiguity of her sex kept us anguished, feverish and exasperated, Monsieur de Mortimer and me, for we always had, dead and alive, the same mistresses— but we preferred the dead for the very inanity of our passion, tempered, like a sword, in the lava and sulfur of despair . . .

"A torment of art, in verity, such was our youth . . . our youth

Prey to vain regrets and vain nostalgias

---

1 Lorrain's fascination with Botticelli's *Primavera*, otherwise known as *The Allegory of Spring*, and with the supposed ambiguity of the sex of the central figure, plays a significant role in some of his other works, notably "Ophélius."

"As I wrote somewhere, in the last tercet of a sonnet, dedicated, if I remember rightly, to Monsieur de Mortimer . . . in fact, yes, I remember it, what a sonnet! I compared him therein, also feeling sorry for myself, to someone ensorcelled by Gothic magic, for that love of specters—are not all portraits specters?—poisons, admit it, the philter and the spell, and I addressed to him, in that sonnet, a grimoire and mirror—for I reflected myself therein—these three lines testifying to our enchantment:

> *Henceforth, obsessed with captivating graces*
> *Of the Dead, insensible to the charms of the Living,*
> *Can your heart find attraction in the past alone,*
> *Edgard?*

"For he was named Edgard, like the laird of Ravenswood, and that Edgard did not lack a Lucy, but it was the Lucy of Nevermore and not of Lammermoor; for, in life as in dreams, his motto, our motto, Messieurs, was that knell of pride: *Nevermore.*[1]

"But how, in truth, can one become infatuated with—what am I saying? how can one even take a slight fancy to—a Museum portrait of one of these fat Dutchwomen? They're béguines,[2] Messieurs, with scant

---

1 Edgar Ravenswood is the hero of Walter Scott's tragic love story *The Bride of Lammermoor* (1819). The refrain "Nevermore," naturally reproduced in English in the original, is from Edgar Poe's "The Raven" (1845), associated with it by sentimental ambiance as well as wordplay.
2 As in members of the lay sisterhood thus nicknamed.

hair and no eyebrows, pink and wishy-washy faces. Have you a taste, by any chance, for that salmon-tinted flesh? Fishwives, they're fishwives—worse, chilblains on wrinkled strawberries . . .

"The rosy hues and nacres of the Flemish school, you'll perhaps object! You make me yawn; they're the rose and nacre of crayfish. The Flemish school is a fish-monger's stall, when there are quarters of fresh meat on the butcher's hooks of Rubens. Talk to me about Velasquez! His infantas might have heads of wax and hair of fleecy silk, but one can be smitten with those dolls. There are reflections of the *auto-da-fé* in the silks and satins of their dresses; and the roses they hold disdainfully in their fingertips, are red with the blood of all the Jews massacred on the steps of cathedrals. And so delightfully scrofulous too! Isn't Velasquez an adequate painter of old aristocracies? There's a sumptu-ous historian of the end of a race of kings.

> *Before a bouffant flood of lampas and silk*
> *Where a pale infanta with slim fingers is sketched,*
> *Relive, in the depths of your sinister palaces,*
> *Your edicts and tragic glories, O kings of Spain.*

"That, Messieurs, is not by Bougrelon, it's by Mortimer. Like me, he had a frantic passion for the Spanish school: Goya, Messieurs, and Coelo, and Antonio Moro, and the most marvelous of all, perhaps, the sublime in the horrible, El Greco, simultaneously infernal and celestial—for the inferno is heaven in excavation. Others have had on their palette the sun,

56

infantile flesh, pearls and roses; El Greco, Messieurs, painted with the blood of wounds; anatomies drawn with hot charcoal, and that charcoal he took from the pyre of the Holy Inquisition. With what somber ardor he makes his heretics blaze on the painting of the Escorial! He was a highly devout Catholic, while these Dutchmen reek of the Reformation.

"Have you visited the church of Saint Bavon in Harlem? It's a sepulcher. It's floored with tombstones; one walks over the dead, and God is absent therefrom. It's like the basilica of Basel. Personally, I hate these protestant peoples with a fervent hatred. Luther is the shadow of this century. Catholicism was red; Protestantism is worse, for it's colorless. It's neutral, and marches through history clad in gray drugget like a peasant. It suppressed the stained-glass of churches, which says it all, and raised women's necklines to the chin; it was the abolition of breasts and saints, of everything that flourishes in the eyes. The flamboyant stained-glass queens in gem-studded robes and naked archangels were a little living heaven in the ogives. The naked cleavages of women projecting from their corsages were a hint of amour, and thus another fragment of paradise, in the gray monotony of days.

"The death of joy, that's what Protestantism has been, Messieurs, and it was also the death of luxury and lust. You'll slap me with Rubens and Van Dyck! I'll reply to you that Rubens was an ambassador; he knew the school of Venice and painted for the Luxembourg the most Italian—what am I saying? the most Florentine—of our queens; I'm referring to Marie de Médicis. As for Van Dyck, he lived in the English court, and the most sumptuous and most elegant of courts, that of the Stuarts, the Valois of Great Britain. Those were, therefore, exceptions; but the others, all those Cornelises, Jans, Peters and Jorises more or less Van den Put or Poters . . . names to lie down outside, admit it, what did they paint? Townswomen and more townswomen, drapers, béguines and burgomasters' wives.

"Only the Spanish painted the daughters of kings, the Italians the mistresses of popes; these good Flemings only really magnified their corporations. Have you visited Harlem? What Franz Halses! The finest, incontestably, but, in sum, they're syndicates, worse, the national guard of that time, for, make no mistake, Messieurs, it's the costume that deludes you, and if those moustached Flemings have swords at their sides, it's as chiefs of militia, not as gentlemen.

"Civic guards, companions of their guild—but great lords, no! And then again, that sword, which seduces you and puts you off the track, they owe to the Spanish conquest. It's the riposte imposed on an entire people in peril, the reply to the permanent scaffolds on the Town Hall Square in Brussels and Herb-Market Square in Antwerp. It was necessary to respond to the Duc d'Albe, and even then, would you dare compare these good Dutch daggers with the fine gold-damascened or iron-annealed swords of the *Surrender of Breda*? Oh, Velasquez, Messieurs, he's my painter!"

And, phantasmal and tragic in the dim light of the small rooms, so expertly regulated, of the Museum,

Monsieur de Bougrelon, pausing in turn before Rembrandt's *Old Woman* and an interior by Gerard Dow, bracing himself emphatically in his Carmelite rhinegraves, brandishing toward the frames the crazy tangle of his frightful muff, perorated, getting carried away with vocal outbursts, silences, poses, theatrical gestures, abruptly striding twenty meters along the gallery, and then suddenly immobile, fixed like a marble statue on the waxed parquet, where, reflected as in dormant water, the enormous rowels of his spurs quivered.

"No, Messieurs," he concluded, with a shrug of his entire upper body, "I can't do it. These bustard faces will never solicit a Bougrelon: a pitiful wardrobe for hanging up the tatters of my dream. But there's something better than paintings here; follow me."

And, abruptly turning on his heel before Rembrandt's *Night Watch*, he took a stairway to the left leading to the ground-floor rooms—a difficult descent because of his old arthritic knees; a slightly macabre descent with his stiff and jerky automaton gait, metal clinking at every step, reminiscent, in that pale January light, of a caricature of the statue of the Commander.

The placid wardens watched us pass by, worthy Dutchmen, exactly similar in their phlegm and their braided coats to the officious doormen of the brothels of the Ness.

"For it's to the brothel that I'm taking you, Messieurs," the old marionette declared to us, "but the brothel of memories; for the women to whose deceptive obsession you are about to be subjected, to the sharpest extremity of desire, you will not even see. I'm taking you to the vestry of the dead, robes empty forever, corsages of nothingness, to the costumes of past centuries, the rags of defunct lovers, because I want to intoxicate you with the dolorous opium of that which might have been and that which is no more.

> *Oh, the challenge of the empty glass*
> *Whose pure and discreet perfume*
> *Only leaves our avid lips*
> *Despair and vain regret."*

And, abruptly lifting a door curtain, he said to us in a strangely softened voice: "Prepare yourselves for all suffering; here we're in the realm of eternal melancholy; it's a boudoir of specters. Look at these display cases—but these specters have left their velvet shrouds and tangible, palpable silks in order to force us to resuscitate them in our memory.

"Here we're in a crypt, and also in an oratory, but a quasi-divine oratory where the Christs surge forth from their frames if we know how to look at them; and they surge forth all the more because there's nothing in these magical frames, nothing but our thoughts and our regrets. They're only rags of silk, lawn and brocade—but how evocative! It's the dust of centuries that we're about to stir; but in that dust, there are kisses, folly, amour and tears. Nostalgic dolls, Messieurs!"

III
Hypothetical Lusts[1]

The vestry of memory! There was a series of rooms illuminated by high windows, with one display-case after another arranged along the walls, vast cupboards of glass, like blocks of ice in which the fashions of defunct centuries appeared to be frozen. Touching preserves of obsolete elegances, they were the so-called costume halls, those in which meticulous Holland keeps and shelters from the dust and the damp the gallant garments, dresses, coats and adornments of preceding reigns; and there were, alongside the long peignoirs with folds imitative of Watteau and country scenes by Pater, thick taffetas, embroideries of silver lilies on a Burgundy wine background, hooped dresses, delicate striped pekins alongside silk sheets, leafy myrtle-green brocades and lustrous satins, as if furrowed with frost, with astragali and love-knots, garlands of eyelets and flowery baskets attached to the fabric by knotted ribbons . . .

Still bulging at the place of the breasts, and flattening at the level of the abdomen, there were the irritating enigma of corsages and skirts; and there were lampases studded with large bouquets red roses on a gold background, sumptuous and heavy fabrics that must once have been worn by the wives of fat bankers and rich

1 The title "Hypothétiques luxures" is reserved for the second of the episodes in *Le Journal* run together in this chapter, the first being entitled "Le Boudoir des Mortes" [The Boudoir of the Dead].

merchants, all the folly of the gold of the counters of Amsterdam, all the crushing luxury of the East India Company, the massive opulence of the insolent benefices of diamond-cutters; visions of enormous cleavages in the style of Jordaens, and hips of slatterns in satins mottled scaled and damascened like armor, strewn with grenadines with split peel, and long pineapples.

Then, beside green resedas paling to sulfur, there were salmon pinks and peach-blossoms, further attenuated by the mist of gauzes and lawns: all the melancholy of the death-throes of the end of the eighteenth century, soft flax blues and dolorous lilacs, shades as if powdered as well as washed by tears, Trianon shepherdesses emigrated to the chilly Netherlands, sentimental Rousseauesque dreams exiled with the nobility of Versailles to the court of the Princes of Orange, discreet and perfumed touches of French elegance that had taken refuge in this country during the Revolution.

Finally, alongside the adornments of women there were men's clothes, Louis XV coats, apartment jackets and court rhinegraves, embroidered and re-embroidered, as florid as flower-beds; long waist coats of changing hues starred with strass, shining with spangles, with the obligatory garlands of narcissi and carnations around the pockets, and royal blue and myrtle green crushed velvet, and the smocks of heroic shepherds, zinzolin and green celadon, evoking the vision of the long, slender torsos of ballet dancers and warrior ephebes, all the pleasures of *L'Île enchantée*,[1] the

---

1 The painting by Watteau (1717).

mythological fêtes of Versailles and masked balls on the frozen ponds of the parks of The Hague.

And as we advanced, slowly and meditatively, past those display-cases reminiscent of sarcophagi, an infinite sadness, a compassionate tenderness, penetrated us, wearying and restful at the same time, and, our limbs seemingly loose, we wandered hither and yon, out of the century, no longer as in a museum, but as in a sick-room, almost fearing to wake the souls in the garments exposed to our gaze.

The boudoir of the Dead: Monsieur de Botrelon had hit upon the right phrase: it was a funereal boudoir, pious and coquettish, as troubling as an alcove but as cold as a sacristy, that the old marionette was showing us around. Instinctively, we had fallen silent; too many phantoms were escorting us; the atmosphere was populated; there were ambushes in every corner.

We were now in front of the headgear: the extravagant, monumental headgear, as bold as challenges, as unexpected as caprices, of the end of the reign of Louis XVI; plumed felt hats turned up by a gust of wind over the edifice of hair raised up in colossal straight roots crowned with roses flourishing around the top of a gigantic Lambale hat, a profound capeline of lawn and silk in which the face of the woman appeared so delightfully refined in the retreat of a niche aureoled with flowers.

Then Monsieur Bougrelon, who had been silent thus far, spoke:

"Do you feel the enchantment of obsolete fashions, the dolorous charm of ancient living things, as I do,

Messieurs? Yes, for I can see you, pallid with a powerful emotion, since it is silent. Did I deceive you when I said: *Prepare yourselves for suffering*? Do not the adorable dead whose vision these adornments impose on you subject you more really to their presence than the varnish or the flatness of a painting?

"Oh, the bewitchment of faded fabrics, the patricienne languor of all these decorations in silk and satin! A church-like atmosphere reigns here, for do you not experience the respect of a holy place? That is because the imperious soul of old aristocracies is floating here, invisible but palpable. What authoritarian grace, what pride there is in the folds of these robes, what innate elegance in their bouffant hoops, what a beautiful audacity in the very ridiculousness of these hats.

"It's an entire vanished society that I rediscover here, for I've known it; I'm at home here. A boudoir of the dead, in truth, but the living dead, for I know the words give body to these rags, I know the words of love and tenderness that reilluminate smiles and gazes here; for these dead women come back—yes, Messieurs, these dead women come back because I love them, and obey me because they know it, for only love resuscitates the dead."

And suddenly leaning on his elbow in a pretentious and inspired pose at the corner of one of the display-cases, Monsieur de Bourgelon removed his large otter-fur hat with the other hand, and pronounced in a declamatory one:

Of old faded fabrics
I am the magnificent lover,
Obsolete colors and fashions,
Who can tell your enchantment?

My soul, which arouses and suffers
Adores the smiles, weary
And fatigued, of sulfur satins
Striped with rose and lilac;

And it is an exquisite adventure
To rediscover in a reflection
The entire blue past of a marquise
Flourishing in jonquil and carnation.

The old lampas with agate tones
Lustrous beneath the talon of time
Has the haughty and delicate
Sadness of distant springs;

The fresh springs of youth,
Aprils gone without return;
Whose lilies of thick silk
Shed their petals in taffeta,

But to sing the intoxication
Errant in this defunct luxury,
Savant and bruising sensuality
Of old kisses and ancient perfumes,

My docile fingers would require
The strings of a viol d'amor
With a hardwood fingerboard
Painted with shepherdesses,

And in the loving and devout shadow
Of an obscure and powdered boudoir
To the dancing tunes of gavottes
Clad in an obsolete costume,

Of old and faded fabrics
I would evoke the charming spirit
And the enchanting dreamer
Of these refined hues!

"Old kisses, old perfumes, old lampas, distant springs, dancing tunes of gavottes, old-fashioned and made-up sexes, luxuries forever abolished . . . yes, all that is my youth, my youth in obsolete garments, faded, as I am myself, an old dandy forgotten in a century of lucre and vulgar appetites, an old marionette taking refuge in the midst of phantoms—that's what I am, Messieurs, in truth."

He paused, out of breath. Make-up was running down his cheeks: two thin furrows of blackened water on the temples and two others at the corners of his lips, the cosmetics of his eyebrows and moustache. Cadaverous under his mixed red and white, at the limit of his strength, collapsed and exhausted in the folds of his rhinegrave, which suddenly seemed too large, Monsieur de Bougrelon, emptier and more ragged than the adornments of nothingness exposed around him, was indeed the pitiful lover of faded fabrics, the macabre and libertine cavalier of that funereal boudoir.

An old scarecrow to put in a field to frighten the birds, that was what our noble and majestic guide to the splendors of the national Museum was.

We took pity on his decrepitude, almost forcing him to sit down on a bench, and having sponged away his sweat with handkerchiefs, we tried to galvanize that poor old cadaver with smelling salts, not without the secret fear of seeing him liquefy in our arms. It would have been too frightful to witness his death-throes in that boudoir of the dead.

Monsieur de Bougrelon was exhausted, by emotion of the fatigue of so much peroration; his upper body oscillated in silence, wedged, so to speak, between the two of us and, his lip slack, he allowed an atonal gaze to float over all those display-cases, where so many follies and amours had been fluttering their wings and whispering a little while ago, resuscitated for him.

Eleven o'clock: the carillon of the old church filled the long halls of the Museum with a faint music, the display-cases vibrating.

"Eleven o'clock! My stomach marks midday," thundered Monsieur de Bougrelon suddenly, as if abruptly woken from his lethargy. "I'll take you to lunch, Messieurs. I know a certain sailors' tavern nearby where you can eat Zeeland oysters, as blonde and fat as the waitresses, and marinaded herrings such as are only made in Groningen. A thousand pardons for having alarmed you with my faint; I'm subject to them when

Barbara speaks to me, and Barbara, as I ought to have told you, always speaks to me in the boudoir of the dead. Will you follow me, Messieurs?"

And we followed on the heels of the old roué. Suddenly cheered up, his figure more braced than ever, as if reanimated by the piquant cold outside, head held high, Monsieur de Bougrelon led the march, incorrigibly, singing to the tune of a gavotte:

> *Of old faded fabrics*
> *I am the magnificent lover.*[1]

"Yes, Messieurs, the fog of these parts brings forth strange fantasies. I've already cited you the case of Lady Barbara Van Mierris; it's one of the most bizarre; but you'll appreciate this haddock. Have you ever felt the flesh of such a fish? How milky it is, and how fresh! One eats marvelously in this matelots' dive, eh? Didn't I tell you so?"

The "matelot's dive" to which Monsieur de Bougrelon had taken us was a shiny and neat steamboat-cabin enclosed, God alone knows why, in the underground cellar of a wooden shack on the quay on the North Sea, at the extremity of the city, behind the central station and the docks, facing the platforms of the steamboats departing for the Zuiderzee and New Holland: a quay of temporary constructions, all hangars and travelers' restaurants with summary roofs of tarred planks, with, even on the causeway, piles of crates and pyramids of

---

1 The episode in *Le Journal* entitled "Le Boudoir des Mortes" ends here

barrels waiting to be loaded, and embarkation pontoons at intervals, the narrow advancement of their piles jutting into the yellow-gray of the North Sea.

A landscape of infinite melancholy, in truth, that of the warehouse quays, with pavements hardened by ice, with its irregular constructions blackened by the smoke and dust of steamers, and a melancholy further aggravated by the solitude of the pontoons and docks, the dinner hour having emptied all the Westel workshops. In the distance, extending for league after league, was the sea the color of hemp and pewter, a shifting sea stirred by an eternal bitter wind that made it alternately gray and yellow, but always livid. On the horizon, there was the garden of the Tolhuis, with its leafless trees and the Northern channel, a long parallelogram cutting into the land with its immutable pallor.

"Three months of residence before that monotonous sea, and the soul shriveled by ennui is ripe for the worst debauches, Messieurs. This land of mists and damp predisposes to anything, and the ugliness of the inhabitants assists with that, for, between us, the types encountered here have superhuman appearances: courgettes and melons, Messieurs, that's for the silhouettes. As for the complexions, they're aubergines; flesh chapped by cold, the Dutch are the people with violet cheeks. Every people, anyway, has the color of a fruit; Spain has the orange tint, feverish Italy is olive-green, and the women of France have the pink down of peaches. Personally, I've always considered women as fruit. Away with insipid comparisons with flowers; flowers are picked, fruits are eaten, and Monsieur de

Mortimer and I always had an appetite before a table set with young women's corsets.

"Anyway, there are women who also reveal themselves as ogresses before the nudity of young men; Barbara was one of those. We met her, Monsieur de Mortmer and I, in Harlem, in the house of an old tulip collector who had invited us to visit his plants; Holland is crazy about horticulture. White, plump, with two mounds of flesh as unctuous as milk, always offered at the window in a corsage of embroidered damask, her hips, which were forceful, swathed in hoops of heavy fabric, and her legs impeded by long and noisy trains, with her collerettes and cherusques of Malines lace and gold guipures, with strings of pearls around her neck, pendant jewels on her forehead and a thousand and one trinkets hanging from her breasts and ears, she was a woman out of Rubens in the full sense of the term: a display-cabinet and a meat-rack, but with a triply wrinkled neck so round and flabby, earlobes so carmined and such a transparency of complexion, and such pearly teeth between the moist pink of her lips, that one wanted to eat that woman with a spoon like a sorbet, Messieurs. She was flavorsome and iced—or at least, she appeared so.

"The widow of a great ship-owner in Rotterdam, and long maintained, it was said, by a prince of the house of Orange, she lived on the bank of a canal, in a sumptuous dwelling composed of three gabled houses and furnished with the ponderous luxury and solid ostentation of the interiors of the country. She wanted to show us round it, but to the enterprises of Monsieur de

Mortimer, who was enticed by that almond milk per-fumed with whisky—for all her flesh was almond milk perfumed with whisky—that truly barbaric Barbara always opposed a firm resistance, as firm as her breasts, which were bastions.

"Dear Edgard made his advances, and I made mine, but we never knew the snowy kiss of her crimson lips—for that damned Dutchwoman had icy breath, Monsieur; when one breathed it in, it was a hedge of eglantine, mountain eglantine half way up a glacier. Oh, that Dutchwoman didn't reek of the swamp, but Monsieur de Mortimer and I did when we were near her, to our brief shame—and shame is a bold antithesis, Messieurs, for our nostalgia was great.

"We remained unable to explain the enigma of that chastity for two years. Barbara had no lover, but if her heart had so decided, her choice would have fallen—so she told us—on Mortimer or me, for she liked us both: an exasperating mystery, that sorbet that did not melt.

> *The irritating, haughty insult*
> *Of snow that does not melt,*
> *That of the distant summit*
> *Inaccessible to footfalls.*

"A mystery of candor and sensuality to which we found the key one day by penetrating the secrets of her bathroom! That soul of snow was hardened against the fire of desires and, to maintain its rigidity, cooked itself in the oven of the most formidable lust, the lust of a negro. Lady Barbara Van Mierris bathed every morning before a colossal Ethiopian.

"By a refinement of carnal cruelty, that white ogress—she was one—had attached that monumental African to her personal service, Messieurs; yes, that negro giant ignited for her the most frantic desires. She had herself laced and shod by him; it was him who lifted her out of the bath, sponged her in her swansdown peignoirs, but prudently clad in bathing-trunks, the trunks of a martyr, Messieurs, in which that man consumed, captive, his frightful desire, sheathed in a prison. It was in the atmosphere of the most tortuous lust that the blonde, plump Dutchwoman blossomed and fortified herself against our enterprises. She lived, avid for emotions, in the perpetual fear of a rape, and took pleasure in observing the eternal threat.

"That naïve child of the desert, with his covetousness always ignited and always brandished over her like a firebrand, was a veritable black statue of insatiable desire. A statue of bronze, Messieurs, every one of whose gazes and gestures made the metal vibrate, and of which she had made the bell-clapper of her ivory tower—the ivory tower in which she lived locked up, protected by that desire, the monstrous pendulum of the clock of her chastity, from ours.

"Hypothetical lust, Messieurs, such as can only be produced by the atmosphere of dreams and fog of these nebulous lands.

"At any rate, that perpetual assault on a modesty offered but inaccessible, concluded with a crime. That incessant torture of Tantalus maddened the tempted negro to such an extent that one evening, the wild beast within the son of the desert woke up roaring; one does not play with tigers with impunity. Lady Barbara Van Mierris was found one morning murdered in her bath, Messieurs, with an enormous gaping wound in her neck and one of her breasts bitten and bloody, torn apart and half-eaten. The negro, enraged by lust, had treated her as a fruit; then the guilty party had fled; but the intact cadaver—you know what I mean—although mutilated, was not the only victim.

"Before killing his beautiful mistress, the Ethiopian, with his murderous hands, had wrung the necks of the Dame Barbara's pet cockatoo and she-monkey, two charming animals—especially the monkey, almost human in its ugliness and simpering, and which, dressed like the best-maintained follower, performed the functions of a maidservant with regard to the blonde Dutchwoman. Paquita was her name, for that she-monkey was an individual, Messieurs, and, dressed up, sometimes in yellow satin and sometimes in orange silk and velvet, her figure tightened at the waist by layered corsets, with enticements like those of a marquise of the last century, deployed a woman's graces and coquetries in the apartments by which Mortimer and I were often troubled—and divinely made up as well, with rouged cheeks and kohl around her eyes. She was more than a doll to Barbara: a child, a friend, the passionately cherished 'little darling' of that truly extraordinary Dutchwoman, who seemed to prefer black to white and animal to human, an icy temperament of abnormal desires.

"But why go on? You've understood me, Messieurs. As to why the negro murdered the she-monkey, calumny dared not even pronounce the word that we have all whispered. The parrot, a white cockatoo with pink-tinted wings, with a beak gilded with powdered gold—Barbara had inconceivable refinements of luxury—had the equivocal mania of pecking the lady's lips and only wanted to eat from her mouth, as it had been trained to do. Paquita did and undid the Dutchwoman's hair every morning and evening. Jealousy armed the negro's hand; I shall say no more about it; we owe respect to the dead, and I loved that madwoman Barbara amorously for five years.

"This ginger conserve, Messieurs, is incomparable in all of Holland; it comes directly from Java."

Nonchalantly leaning back in his chair, Monsieur de Bougrelon had taken from the depths of his rhinegrave a box of powder and cosmetics, a comb and a sculpted silver pocket mirror, curiously worked, believe me, with pink topazes and moonstones embedded in the metal.

"Quite pretty, this mirror, isn't it, with its lunar mounting—but lunar in the twilight? With these pink topazes and selenites, isn't it the rising of Diana in the setting sun? It came to me from Barbara, Messieurs; it's her she-monkey's mirror."

And without deigning to notice the mad giggling that we imparted at that connection, the old beau, imperturbably, powdered his cadaverous face, heightened with rouge the nostrils of his eagle's-beak nose, his dry thin lips and the parchment of his cheeks, waxed the stiff points of his moustache, touched up his eyebrows and the corners of his lashless eyes with pencil, replastered the ruins of his aged visage and replenished his centenarian beauty with unguents.

Outside, there was cold and ice, the unpolished vitreous sky of misty Holland, the waves the color of hemp, and those the color of pewter, of the restless North Sea . . .

"Hypothetical lust, Messieurs.[1] Hypothetical lust!"

✳

"It's very Flemish, and particular to these Northern souls, that effervescence of cerebral rut, leading instinct astray and crossing the boundaries of species and sex. Holland doesn't have a monopoly on it; Belgium is ravaged by it, Messieurs, and without dwelling on the orgiastic painting of the Antwerp school . . . and the debauchery of the fairgrounds of Teniers, which I'd forgotten . . . there isn't only Bruges-la-sainte, Bruges, that ivory and gold reliquary, mirroring in the tinplate of its canals, its precious miniatures of Van Eyck and Memling, there isn't only Bruges, Bruges that is said to be dead and is only sleeping, which coddles, swaddled in mystical linen, the most titillating priapism, that of béguines!

"Have you visited Bruges? And the bells of the tower in Bruges? A nuns' dormitory, Messieurs, and nuns of bronze, whose orison that bell-tower hums. The carillons are the litanies of those kneeling virgins. Even silent, they're urns murmuring dreams, for they're souls, Messieurs. They've been baptized, and the bell-ringer who sets their troop in motion, and makes the orison

---

1 The episode in *Le Journal* ends here; the next is entitled "Fantastique manchon" [A Fantastic Muff].

of their metal flesh spring forth, is their confessor, and never their lover. Well, in Bruges-la-sainte there was a man, a Belgian, a Fleming who desired and solicited the love of bronze bells. The fact is historic, Messieurs; in Bruges, his name is spoken.

"An unprecedented case of hypothetical lust, which will perhaps inspire some novelist of the future, that Boorluut—his name comes back to me now—loved his bells like young women, like prostitutes, Messieurs, and obtained in agitating them the same sensual and sexual voluptuousness for which you and I need whores, to the extent that that bell-tower in Bruges had become a vessel of lust, Messieurs, and the carillons of those culpable bells, quivering with lust and desire, had ended up corrupting the city; and, as Monsieur de Mortimer said, it isn't Boorluut but Horrut that the bold cavalier of brazen rumps should have been named.[1]

"That story, Messieurs, will not excuse, in your view, but will at least facilitate the comprehension of the strange adventure into which Monsieur de Mortimer and I allowed ourselves to slide, even here in Holland. We did not love bells, no, but our lust, hypothetical as it was, might seem to you to be worse. You will judge, when you have heard me, the extremity to which two magnanimous souls might descend, or rise, when di-

---

1 Boorluut is a deliberate corruption of Borluut, the protagonist of *Le Carillonneur* [The Bell-Ringer] (1897; tr. as *The Bells of Bruges*) by Georges Rodenbach, whose earlier Decadent classic, *Bruges-la-morte*, is also referenced in the passage, it's title being deliberately parodied in the improvised epithet Bruges-la-sainte.

lapidated by ennui: ennui, ferocious ennui; ennui as mordant as an acid; ennui, the circle of lead that the eternal weight of this dismal gray sky puts around the temples. Yes, the fog of these Netherlands drives one, in verity, to bizarre fantasies."

And, turning up his stiff dyed moustache with the deft, nonchalant and proud gesture of a king's musketeer: "I've already told you, Messieurs, how dear that Barbara Van Mierris was to us. White, plump and blonde, the silvery blonde of the Spanish infantas or well-bred spaniels, that divine woman combined with so many other charms the incomparable attraction of two liquid green eyes—not the green of emerald, no, but the green of absinthe, and a defeated absinthe, the milky and transparent green of peridot. Whoever has not known those eyes is ignorant of the color of philters. They were a philter, Messieurs, and a black philter, a philter of darkness, the gaze of Astarté, the eye of lust itself, the one that I have often seen in dreams in the plaster eyes of the Antinous.[1]

"That Barbara we had adored in life. That tells you whether we idolized her in death . . .

---

1 The reference is to a large bust of Antinous—the Emperor Hadrian's Greek catamite, deified on the emperor's orders—on display in the Louvre, sometimes known as the Antinous Mondragone. Lorrain had previously associated it with the sinister gaze of Astarté in his novelette "Un démoniaque" (1895; tr. as "One Possessed"), which was later adapted as the core of the novel *Monsieur de Phocas. Astarté.* Lorrain's preoccupation with the motif might well derive from an actual dream; he continued to suffer from nightmares long after he had stopped taking ether as a stimulant.

"On cold winter days, when Monsieur de Mortimer and I were parading the incurable ennui of our exile along the frozen canals or these deserted quays, they fluttered before us like nostalgic fire follets, those transparent and glaucous eyes of the most desirable of Dutchwomen . . .

"Now, one morning in January on which, attempting to distract our melancholy, Mortimer and I had decided to go scrape the ice off our skates in the Marken Islands[1] . . . by the way, you must, Messieurs go to visit that island; the costume of the local women is flavorsome; you'll love, as I do, the short skirts of scarlet fabric and legs like Diana in gaiters, and along with that, golden antennae projecting from beneath headdresses like aureoles . . . an epic coiffure, Messieurs, half Japanese and half Flemish, which will cause your livers to swell with delight: a béguine's cornet and a Samurai's helmet; those fisherwomen of Marken Island are as many little Salomes with their short skirts and their shiny diadems; red as lady-apples too, Messieurs, hard nipples and eyes like dirty water . . . oh, that island has benefits, and I don't mourn its fishermen . . .

"So, we were wandering, Monsieur de Mortimer and I, along the quays of Monnikendam—Monnikendam

---

1 When the story was written, Marken was still an island, or group of islands, in the Zuiderzee—it has since been connected to the mainland—and had recently attracted intense interest from ethnographers because its people were regarded as the last surviving relic of a traditional native culture that was on the brink of disappearing, as it was finally caught up by the tide of progress and cultural fusion.

is the port of embarkation for Marken—having dined there on a brandade of cod and goose in anchovy paste, a culinary delicacy of the region, and we were roaming along the quays, as I said, a trifle disappointed because of the heavy blocks of ice floating in the harbor. We had thought we would be able to get to Marken by skating—an error, Messieurs; the ice had insufficient purchase and the sea, meanwhile, was carrying such floes that it would have been folly to risk it in a boat. In any case, no fisherman would have lent us his boat; the trip had, therefore, to be postponed, and like the true Frenchmen we were, we were cursing that ill-luck, with sullen expressions, when Barbara's watery green eyes suddenly illuminated before us . . .

"Those eyes, they were her eyes, and we weren't drunk on schiedam—it was only two o'clock—and the eyes were staring at us; better than that, they were smiling at us and challenging us, Messieurs, and those eyes—you'll shiver when I've told you—those eyes were those of a dog, a frightful street-dog, a white mongrel soiled with soot and coal-dust. It wasn't even a spaniel, a delightful King Charles as painted by Landseer, one of those delightful little beasts of luxury, as wisps of silvery blonde silk, the silvery blonde that Barbara, alive, had carried in her silver-blonde hair; it was a wretched and sordid mongrel; but under its tangled fur there was the magnet of two liquid green eyes, a green so glaucous and so phosphorescent that . . . without saying a word, Monsieur de Mortimer and I looked at one another— what a gaze!—and, frightened, the green-eyed mongrel abruptly ran off.

"We followed it. It ran before us, crestfallen, its tail between its legs; we followed it—pursued it, in fact. Oh, the fog of these Netherlands and its deleterious influence on souls in exile! We chased the beast outside the suburbs. 'I sense the soul of a negro in me,' Monsieur de Mortimer said to me then. My God, I can still see it: the fearful mongrel looked at us with its great imploring eyes; unfortunately, they were the green of young shoots, a green of almond and reeds . . .

"We took the unfortunate little beast to a hairdresser, Messieurs, who soaped it, bathed it, perfumed it with bergamot and *eau de Portugal,* and, after many shampooings—a bagatelle of ten florins!—returned to us, curled and flowery, the most delightful white lap-dog—fortunately, it was a bitch—that a duchess painted by Gainsborough might have dreamed of putting on her footstool. Monsieur de Mortimer, enthused, immediately bought a collar of turquoises and called it Barbara . . .

"It's her fur I'm carrying," Monsieur de Bougrelon suddenly ejaculated, standing up violently, "but her fur dyed black as a sign of mourning, for I won't hide it from you that Barbara met a bloody end; that name predestined it. Barbara was murdered, and by virtue of jealousy, like the Other; she had to be murdered.

"Monsieur de Mortimer was her negro; he had suffered too much by virtue of the one whose memory she imposed upon him; the present avenged the past; one day, he could no longer bear the obsessive illusion of the eyes, and he cut the throat of the unfortunate pooch . . . unfortunate and innocent.

"Of her bloody fur, I had this muff made, Messieurs, dyed black beforehand. I've thought for some time of casting negligently into these long dark tresses two peridots, or two pale emeralds, which would have reminded me of her gaze, but that would have been too funereal a lust, and in any case, I found her phosphorescent and troubled gaze, those diabolically green irises, that nostalgic and glaucous philter, once again, in the soul of Atala."[1]

We were dealing with a madman; this time, Monsieur de Bougrelon had exceeded all measure; he was abusing us. He did not say much more that day; our host stood up; we had already been at table for five hours, and in the fog, the rare street-lamps were beginning to light up along the quays. It was the time when the noble lady who wished him well was waiting for the old exile from Avranches. He dined with that beautiful lady every evening, and played his game of ombre with her. All of the old gentleman's evenings belonged to that friend of bad days.

In consequence, Monsieur de Bougrelon stood up, put on his hat, turned up the collar of his rhinegrave,

---

1 The reference to *l'ame d'Atala* [the soul of Atala] would immediately have put a contemporary reader in mind of Chateaubriand's classic novella *Atala* (1801), a monument of the Romantic movement, and a specific passage in which the protagonist invokes the soul of the ill-fated Amerindian heroine Atala three times, evoking an equivocal response from the Genius of the Desert. Some readers mistook Chateaubriand's work as a celebration of Jean-Jacques Rousseau's thesis regarding the essential virtue of pre-civilized innocence rather than a criticism of it, but Lorrain was too intelligent a reader to make that mistake.

and, with an aristocratic wave of the fingertips, took his leave of us. According to his habit, he left us to settle the bill.

On the threshold: "You won't see me tomorrow, Messieurs; I'll have the regret of doing without your company. Tomorrow, I'll be fully occupied with my devotions; I assist at mass and at vespers, in the private chapel of the Dutch lady who claims me every evening, for tomorrow is Sunday. Until Monday then, Messieurs."

And like a phantom, vertiginous and macabre, that extraordinary man pirouetted on the spot and evaporated, *pfft!* into the darkness of the great deserted quay.

It smacked of prodigy; one might have thought that he had fallen into the night.

The next day was rather dismal. Oh, the sadness of Sundays abroad! We returned to the Museum, visited the Fodor collection,[1] whose out-dated name was, in verity, the only thing that pleased us, and about five o'clock, as we were walking through the narrow and populous streets of the Seadeck—the marine quarter—amused by the dives, whose horn windows lit up one by one at nightfall, we thought we perceived, stealing away cautiously and slyly, the green frock-coat of our guide.

---

1 The Museum Fodor was opened in 1863 to display the collection of paintings, mostly by Flemish artists, assembled by the coal-merchant Carel Joseph Fodor (1801-1860), which he bequeathed to the city. The collection was eventually taken over by the Amsterdams Historisch Museum and no longer has a separate existence.

Oh, that was not the fine, impertinent and rebellious gait of the Bougrelon we knew. He had nothing of the leading man, the captain of the day before, that poor old man with the gliding and furtive step, his head sunk between his shoulders, who hastened his pace and hugged the walls, as if shrinking in order not to be seen. No, it could not be him; the glimpsed silhouette was carrying a package under his arm wrapped in a sheet, an oblong package such as musicians carry who are going to play in the city. The long fingerboard of an instrument, a violin or guitar, protruded from the parcel.

Furthermore, the man was not alone; an old woman swathed in a vast shawl was trailing in his wake, painfully curbed beneath the weight of a harp. It was a couple of poor ambulant musicians; we had evidently made a mistake . . .

In any case, the man and the woman had almost immediately been swallowed up by the wall; scarcely had they appeared than they had vanished, as if fallen into the ventilation-shaft of a cellar . . . and we had the shock of a new suspicion at that abrupt disappearance, that phantasmal vanishing so similar to the quasi-spectral exits of Monsieur de Bougrelon. But there are stranger resemblances, and more impressive encounters, and we continued our doleful tour of the dives of the Seadeck, amused by our mistake, and even slightly intrigued by a hypothesis whose reality would not have displeased us.

IV
The Soul of Atala[1]

On Monday, Monsieur de Bougrelon did not reappear; we kicked our heels for two hours without seeing the alarming silhouette of the individual in question surge into the vestibule of the hotel. War-weary, we decided on an excursion to Sarrdam, for it is necessary to conform to the itinerary of the guide-books, and a day in Sarrdam is entirely indicated, with a visit to the house of Peter the Great[2]—but how could we make ourselves understood in that accursed half-English and half-German idiom that is the Dutch language?

With our inexperience in the language, it was so difficult, such a song-and-dance, to obtain the necessary information, that we missed the departure of the steamboat by ten minutes. It was therefore necessary for us to wait for an hour on that bitterly cold warehouse quay, exposed to all the winds—and all the winds were blowing and whistling that day on the channel of the North Sea; those waves the color of hemp and pewter had never been so restless, never had the melancholy of that land of dream and fog been more poignant. Oh,

---

1 Again, "L'Âme d'Atala" is reserved for the second of the two episodes from *Le Journal* run together in this chapter; the first is entitled "Visions d'art" [Visions of Art].

2 I have retained Lorrain's spelling of the name of the city then known as Saardam and now as Zaandam, where the house in which the Russian Czar stayed for a week in 1697, attempting unsuccessfully to remain *incognito*, is still preserved as a museum-piece.

that day we had the bleak and incurable depressing sensation of our exile . . .

Our usual interpreter was missing; Amsterdam was no longer Amsterdam without Monsieur de Bougrelon; he was the *raison d'être* of the dreary wintry décor of icy canals and houses with black and white gables; he was its gaiety and its fantasy, and it was through the excess of his heroic imaginations that we had loved the monotony of its streets and the truly hostile ugliness of its inhabitants.

That hostility had never offended us as much as it did that day, and in our distress, we took pleasure in repeating the phrases with which our regretted guide had stigmatized that ugliness the day before. "Courgettes and melons for silhouettes, and aubergines for complexion, Messieurs; their flesh chilled by cold, the Dutch are the people with violet cheeks. As for the types encountered, swathed in furs and coiffed with bonnets, they're seals; they vary, Messieurs, between dried fish and sea-cows. Calverstraat, their main street, is named the street of calves; they are doing themselves justice; they're veal-calves, Messieurs."

Not that there was not a certain exaggeration in those words, but the exaggeration in question was not calculated to displease us that day; it shored up our lassitude and reanimated our souls, extenuated by ennui. We decided to leave that very evening, but resolved before then to return to Harlem to see the Frans Halses again. That would be the employment of the day; we would come back in the evening to pack our trunks.

Scarcely had we reached the station, however, than a fine rain began to fall, and the downpour no longer let us alone. It wove damp darkness on the windows of the carriage, drowned the phantom windmills and dried-up reed-beds of the landscape; it was the most miserable expedition. We found Harlem sullen in the rain, a Harlem of empty streets, with steaming shop-fronts under a sky of soot melted by torrential inundations.

A sumptuous berline, official, to judge by the livery of its coachman, trailed us around from museum to museum, all the way to the town hall, the sage-old casket of the treasure of Harlem. Under the incessant downpour, however, drumming the windows and crackling on the titles, the Franz Halses left us rather cold. Appearing in the livid daylight of an excessively neat and polished aquarium, all the objects in display-cases, all the aldermen and civic guards, caressed our eyes inexpressively; they lacked the prestigious cicerone that Monsieur de Bougrelon would have been.

We dined poorly in a kind of tavern situated facing Saint Bavon: "A Lutheran cathedral," our regretted guide would have said, "whose empty aspect and icy nudity claw the soul." In that tavern we substantiated ourselves with a lukewarm, apathetic and insipid nourishment in harmony with the landscape; the sauces there were colorless, the fish devoid of bones and the meat bland. Only the ginger preserves fortified us— but in order to wipe our fingers we had a luxury of paper napkins, and the plates were old Delft, the faience of which was imprinted with French words: *Bonjour, Monsieur, Bonjour.*

A strange land, where the plates talk like parrots!

The fish-market, with fishwives coiffed in top hats over lace bonnets, solicited us briefly; fishmongers are marvelous in the Netherlands, every stall, with the nacres and bright silvers of its merchandise, forms a tableau there—and that was our day in Harlem, where we did not see any tulips.

And that rain was still falling; we found ourselves back in Amsterdam, where we arrived back sooner than we had anticipated; the hours in Harlem have a hundred and twenty minutes, and one shortens them.

Amsterdam was lit up when we arrived. With the glare of the shop-fronts, the gaslight at the street-corners and the electric projections of beacons, our lassitude dissipated. The swarming Calverstraat, furrowed by the comings and goings of chubby Dutchmen and cheerful Dutchwomen with large rumps and forceful bosoms, circulating ponderously under the pitter-patter of the rain, whipped up our nerves and, beginning to recover a taste for life, we began to stroll, amused and curious, before the displays, ablaze with light, of fashion boutiques and diamond merchants.

Amid all those dazzling things, we stopped in front of a sumptuous store selling furs and travel equipment, of which the Dutch have the refinement. There were toiletry bags and handbags, displaying the brown of pigskin, the velvety gray of the most supple deerskin, with the nickel and silver of exquisite trimmings. There were also valises like works of arts, with buckles and hooks of fine steel on the straps, and such a wide range of color and grain in the leather that the display became a disconcerting and tender vision: an immediate request for intimate contact, for sly stroking.

An idea of nudity emerged therefrom, imperiously; the gaping dives of the Ness were less suggestive of the intoxication of flesh. Furs—marten, mink and sable—cast over the objects, further exaggerated their obscenity: silky shadows of long blonde and brunette tresses that one might have thought were shaven human fleeces, or pubic hair, perverse and discreet touches posed to those bare skins; and all those furs and all that tanned leather was tempting, caressing, enticing.

"Do you have negro souls? Ah—I've surprised you here, Messieurs; you too are subject to the deleterious influence of this depressing foggy country. Hypothetical lusts are aflame in your eyes, in your quivering hands, in the fever of your attitude. Monsieur de Mortimer and I had that blue gimlet gaze as we purchased the unfortunate white lap-dog in Monnikendam, whose fur muff I was wearing yesterday."

It was Monsieur de Bourgrelon, abruptly surging forth behind us, from who knows where and who knows how, a varnished, polished Monsieur de Bougrelon newly painted and replastered, cheeks rosy and moustache waxed: a corseted and braced Monsieur de Bougrelon, wrapped in a black velvet spencer like a German student. His long neck of an old eagle emerged from a foam of old russet lace; green and blue stones negligently dotted around that collaret, false sapphires and false emeralds—for if they had been real the old marionette would have had ten thousand florins on him—completed that adornment of a perfect charlatan.

Holding a dandy's lorgnon in his right hand at eye-level, Monsieur de Bougrelon smiled, indolently camped on his right hip, his crossed legs forming a kind of pedestal for his upper body. With the other hand he was leaning on an enormous cane with a gold pommel, a kind of "executive power" such as characters in Vernet carry—and it was, in truth, a Vernet that the heroic Monsieur de Bougrelon incarnated that day, under the lashing rain.[1]

"And you would be stupid, Messieurs—and worse, impotent—if you had resisted the velvety, soft and ticklish charm of these tanned hides and the aggravated suppleness of the furs. What temptation there is in that display, Messieurs! In France one would not stop; there are Frenchwomen in the streets; but here, the humid atmosphere and the oblique light are envelopments so caressing that objects are lubricated here, Messieurs. These handbags and furs are the entirety of the Dutch school; here there are no dead natures, for the dead natures are alive. Do you understand Monsieur de Mortimer now?"

And as we made as if to draw away slightly embarrassed—for a crowd was beginning to gather around us—the old madman, pointing with the tip of his cudgel at a traveling rug in waterproof fabric, lined with I know not what unfamiliar pelt, all long silvery and silky

---

1 The reference is presumably to Horace Vernet (1789-1863) rather than to his father or grandfather, who were also painters; he developed a more naturalistic style, taking many of his subjects from contemporary culture, including portraits of dandies as well as the battle scenes for which he was most celebrated.

tresses, the silvery blonde of spaniel's ears: "Barbara's hair, Messieurs, had that softness and that hue."

And indicating with his lorgnon a Tibetan goatskin: "The very fur of Barbara, Messieurs, Barbara the pooch, the Other—do you grasp the relationship? And the evident recollection of identical sensations by the two objects? Two objects . . . I'm expressing myself badly, Messieurs: two individuals, for there are no objects in Holland, there are only visions.

"But people are listening to us, it seems to me; the peasants are doing us that honor. Let's have a change of air, Messieurs, we've brought enough custom to the place; French taste makes the law here; we've stopped in front of this display, the merchant's fortune is made." And, passing his arm familiarly under mine, Monsieur de Bougrelon took us away from Calverstraat.

"A schiedam, Messieurs, you'll take a schiedam? I have two hours to give you before going to the rendezvous that you know, in the home of the Lady . . . a Lady of beauty, Messieurs, to whom I shall have to introduce you one of these evenings; she possesses the most curious collection of conserves."

"Conserves?"

And as we pulled up: "Precisely: conserves—for here, Messieurs, conserves are true visions of art. I know bottles of Chinese pickles and apricots, Messieurs, that make Van Ostades pale by comparison. Rubens alone—or, better, Van Dyck alone—could contest the flesh-pinks and silver sheens of certain bottles of anchovies and marinated oysters, Messieurs! Their ragged and pale aspect, that decomposing lint—one might think them fetuses—what a poem! All the sabbats of Goya, those bottles of oysters contain. They're stillborn children offered by witches to Mamoun, the demon king. I won't insist on the green phallophories suggested by bottles of asparagus.[1] What a reliquary of memories for a courtesan! And the citrons, the round towers of glass in which the roundness of citrus fruits sleeps, piled up, like silks . . . oh, those firm citrons, closed, flavorsome, perfumed, simultaneously breasts and peaches, fruit and flesh; it's in the boudoir of the Dead, before the eternally empty corsages of the costume museum, that it's necessary to consume them, one by one.

"Hypothetical gluttony, yes, Messieurs, and the marvelous hues, the glaucous, yellow and green luminosities of those conserves are as many visions of art! I've told you and I repeat, the most gripping nostalgia of all is perhaps in bottles of vegetables and fruits. The vegetal first—what a source of the fantastic! The old Flemish painters understood that well, who introduced in their *Sabbats* and their *Temptations*, in the anatomy of their devils and the composition of their monsters, all the vegetables and fruits in creation.

"Do you remember the Hieronymus Bosch in the museum of Brussels; try to recall your memories, to evoke the painting representing the great combat of the angels and the demons. There are evil spirits figured there, some as leeks and one as a turnip winged like a bee, that are equal in horror to all the phantasma-

1 In Ancient Greece phallophories, or phallogoges, were solemn processions in honor of Dionysus, in which an enormous wooden phallus was transported in procession.

gorias of wyverns and dragons; and the famous frog whose open belly displays the interior of a grenadine—what unexpectedness in terror, what comicality in abomination![1] That terror and that horror can, since they belong to art, become seduction and charm, and to that seduction, to that attraction, even, you too will be subject, when you visit my Lady's collection. You caught fire like vine-branches in front of that shop just now; I'm certain of you—you'll melt before the soul of Atala."

"The soul of Atala?"[2]

"The soul of Atala is a pineapple, Messieurs, a pineapple bathing in its juice, a pineapple in a jar of preserves—but what a pineapple, what a jar and what juice! When we discovered it, Monsieur de Mortimer and I, in the shop window of a merchant of comestibles on the Dam, we were suddenly inundated with light in the depths of our souls. It was radiant, that jar, like a monstrous emerald in which a fruit with golden palms was fixed. That pineapple, Messieurs, was entirely Barbara's eyes, and also the depths of the sea.

"Vertiginous and glaucous, it contained the whole Atlantic, Messieurs, and the whole Pacific and all of the Indies, and America too. It was I know not what

---

1 The Bosch painting cited is *The Fall of the Rebel Angels* but the frog with the open belly is in Pieter Bruegel the Elder's similarly-titled version of the same subject.
2 The episode in *Le Journal* ends here.

transparent and green vision steeped and shadowed and sunlit, a vision re-remembered through algae, the reflections of masts and rigging, moving algae, sunken rigging and lost reflections—*the depths of the sea*, as I've already told you. All the dolors, all the regrets of projected departures, aborted dreams, unslaked joys also floated in that jar. Nostalgic and mysterious, it was a place of dreams haunted by specters and wrecks; there were very ancient shipwrecks within it, and phantoms of dead amours. The leaves of the pineapple, like slow green pendulums, and the pineapple itself, grimacing and fixed behind the walls of glass, were animated there, becoming in the shadows as many strange beings, whose motionless life was disquieting.

An abyss, that jar, Messieurs, and better than that, *the* abysm, the abysm and its undulating and green-tinted nightmare, the abysm imprisoned in walls of glass; and the soul of voyages, the soul of distant lands, that of the distant Americas and Indies, the soul of Java, Sumatra and the Fortunate Isles, the isles one never attains—the soul of Atala, in sum, for that name summarizes everything—captive with the gulf in the apparent banality of a pickle-jar; all the sublime *Invitation au voyage*,[1] all of Baudelaire in a grocer's display!

"That's what that pineapple was, Messieurs!

"Monsieur de Mortimer and I did not hesitate; we never hesitated, even before mongrels. We went into the grocer's shop and we bought that jar.

"For a long time, it ornamented the lodgings that Monsieur de Mortimer and I had for our place of tor-

---

1 The classic poem by Baudelaire from *Les Fleurs du mal*.

ment, a few steps away from Admiral Ruyter's house in the fog and wind of Prince Henry's Quay. A delightful retreat, Messieurs, that abode enriched by us, especially by him, with the luxury and artistic expertise of the taste of a great aristocrat—for he was that to a greater extent than anyone else in the world. He was the last, in fact, and I truly regret that you never knew him; he would have captured you with his charm, you would have been snared by the birdlime of his manners; he had elevated and charming manners, and merely seeing him walk, stand up and sit down, without even open-ing his mouth, would have been a bath of delights for you, a taste of elegance and the good life, of which your nephews, Messieurs, will have no suspicion.

"That dear Edgard had spent five years of his child-hood in London, and it sprang to the eyes that he had known Brummell, King George and Buckingham.[1] He was, in truth, one of the only men of the century, and if my heart is broken by regrets in thinking of what a friend I have lost, it is a source of pride to me, Messieurs to have been his companion in exile, the impavid and

1 George Brummell (1778-1840) and Richard Temple-Grenville (1776-1839), who was later to become the Marquess of Bucking-ham when that title was re-created for him, were both members of the coterie formed around the Prince of Wales who was eventually to become George IV (1762-1830) in the early years of the nine-teenth century, and which set the fashion of male dress. Brummell became legendary as the model of the new style, although its true author was Lord Byron. It is not clear how Monsieur de Mortimer, even if he was ten years older than Monsieur de Bougrelon, could possibly have known them; it is presumably another artifact of Monsieur de Bougrelon's elastic sense of duration.

faithful Patroclus of that Norman with the profile of Achilles."

And, pouring himself another glass of schiedam: "He was full of charming anecdotes; the majority of them he had lived. The society in which we moved was not exactly today's assembly of boors. Would you like an example? A great noise is made in the newspapers about the hunts hosted by the financiers of our day; they're the aristocrats of modern times—a pitiful epoch, Messieurs, and an even more pitiful society, in which money is everything.

"Well, when Monsieur de Mortimer and I were running red deer in mid-autumn—deer or wild boar, for we were great lovers of the hunt—on the estate of the Vidame de Gondrecourt, whose income was rather paltry, scarcely sixty thousand a year, and whose nobility quite recent, only dating back to Louis XII, but do you know how guests were treated in that little vidamat in Poitou? On hunting mornings , at four o'clock sharp, twenty young dressmakers, twenty seamstresses, twenty young Poitevines as fresh as lady-apples, dressmakers from the town invaded the guest-rooms and briskly, with their nimble fingers, thimbles on their thumbs and thread in their mouths, sewed us alive into our hide culottes; we were sheathed point for point in our pumiced deerskin, Messieurs, and so precipitately that they sometimes pricked us in the buttocks, and we were so stiff, thus trousered, that it sometimes required two men to plant us in the saddle like picadors.

"An hour of riding and we were supple, but so tightly-clad in our deerskin and our legs so closely stuck to the flanks of our mounts that we were all one, ourselves, our trousers and our stallions.

"And what a hunt, Messieurs! No crowds of beaters frightening the prey and driving it toward you, weak-legged and bloodless with terror, almost minced flesh. Three dog-handlers, two whippers, and all horn-blowers—that was sufficient for twenty men. We were mounted by five o'clock, once mass was said to the dogs, before going into the woods; at eight we flushed out the beast; at ten we had breakfast in Poitiers, just time to let the horses breathe, and in the evening, at six, we sounded the halloo under the walls of Vienna—Vienna in Austria, Messieurs![1]

"An archduke was waiting for us there—that was the hunts of old! Yes, that's the way it was, and in the evening, at midnight, we were waltzing with the Empress at the Court ball; but our hide trousers were cooked. In our day, deerskin trousers were only worn twice."

And, sponging his face with ragged lace, for Monsieur de Bourgelon had run so hard in his imagination from Poitiers in Poitou to Vienna in Austria that the dear fellow was hot and the make-up sweating along his moist cheeks in large droplets, he went on: "He was a prestigious man, of inexhaustible verve, and when I've told what happened to him in Avranches with a certain Madame de Mertigny, a rather mature beauty but full of pretention, you'll like him, as I did.

"Among other advantages—for he was as handsome as a Greek god, Monsieur de Mortimer had the slim-

---

1 The distance between Poitiers and Vienna is 1218 kilometers (757 miles).

mest waist, the most supple and shapely; and his waist, like a wasp or an Opéra dancer, had already been worth more than ten duels to him, as many with civilians as officers in the guards, for that extravagant slenderness—more than extravagant, implausible, confusing and misleading—enraged all men and, needless to say, offended all women . . . no, only those that Mortimer treated with indifference; but Madame de Mertigny was one of those.

"Haughty and formal with his peers, Monsieur de Mortimer treated the humble with a charming urbanity; he was even familiar sometimes, but with an exquisite familiarity that seemed to be asking for pardon from people for dominating them, and made all those who served him adore him. Lauzun in the salons but Beaufort in the servants' parlor, when he was in Avranches, Monsieur de Mortimer, although he had a full household, valets for the bedroom, valets for the table and more for the dogs, had the habit of having his fires lit and his hot water brought up by an old seamstress long employed by his family, a terrible duenna, one-eyed, hump-backed and lame who made one ill to look at her, Messieurs, but who adored that great fool Edgard fanatically.

"She had seen him as a child, and childhood is the age of the heart, when it doesn't grow old.

"That Mère Nidouille—for that gnome in a skirt had that grotesque name—lived in Avranches on an income left to her by a Mortimer. Edgard called her his last passion, and in the morning, when the frightful Nidouille, limping along and drooling, came into the room of that Homeric god, he took pleasure in interrogating her from the depths of his big bed on the trivial incidents and opinions of the town, and confessed the old servant regarding the scandals of the society.

"Now, one morning in January, to his usual question: 'Well, Madame Nidouille, what are they saying in Avranches this morning?' the old gorgon, in her falsetto voice, replied: 'They're saying, Monsieur de Mortimer, that you wear a corset.' Then he, suddenly sitting up straight, and vibrant: 'Ah! They're saying that I wear a corset! And who says that, Madame Nidouille?' 'Madame Mertigny, in the corner of the square.' 'Ah! Madame Mertigny claims that I wear a corset! Well, you tell her, Madame Nidouille, that it's in for repair, my corset. You can also tell her, that with or without a corset, de Mortimer—me, Edgard—has ten centimeters less than her around the waist, and that I can prove it . . . or rather, no, don't say anything at all. Oh, that gossip claims that I wear a corset, does she? I'll make hers burst, or amour is no longer my master.'

"And he did as he said. Although that Mertigny was past thirty-five and only just becoming, still accommodated to *eau de lys* and tapped by the milliner, Mortimer courted her, broke through her rancid virtue, conquered her and impregnated her, and when the slanderer, once well pregnant had a spoiled figure and, on the point of giving birth, wanted to keep to her room, spending her days sprawling on her sofa, Mortimer went to see her, his figure strapped up under his rhinegrave in one of the beauty's corsets—she had forgotten several in his house—and, the hand once kissed, the news obtained and the lap-dog stroked, Mortimer suddenly stood up and, parting his rhinegrave with a flick: 'You have said, Madame, that I wear a corset; I ought, by virtue of gallantry, not to make you a liar, but it has been necessary for me to take one of yours, not knowing the addresses of the men who make these machines. But see the extremity to which you have driven me in forcing me to fatten you up in order to take it! You no longer wear one, and it's me who is in a sheath. But deign to remark that the sheath doesn't render me uncomfortable.' That's the kind of man that Monsieur de Mortimer was.

"How he loved that soul of Atala! How he looked at it, especially! His verve in that regard was admirable; he never wearied of it. It was a sea of glass eternally warm, forests of madrepores and violet pendulums, many strange beings seen through the glass. 'Look,' he often said to me, his eyes fixed on the jar, 'the shadow of tall sailing ships is passing over the dahlias of submarine forests; at this moment I'm in the shadow of whalers heading for the pole![1] At this moment, stevedores are unloading vessels laden with ice in the harbor.' And there were walruses and seals that he could see swimming backwards in the green water of coves; sea-cows as hairy as women and as pink as girls revealed themselves to him in grottoes; then he left for Java, striding

---

1 This sentence is a direct quotation of two lines from a poem by Maurice Maeterlinck, "Cloche à plongeur" [The Diving Bell] published in *Serres chaudes* (1889), and several of the other lines from the poem are quoted, paraphrased or varied slightly in this passage.

back and forth on terraces where the sea breezes stirred banana plantations and supple palm-trees with a calm rhythm, like as many fans, and there were the perfidious and peppery suggestions of the lands of Asia, the golden cities of India, and the priestesses of Indra.

"That soul of Atala, we had to part with, when de Mortimer, ruined by the death of his uncle de Blessemcourt, suddenly found himself deprived of his income: eighty thousand livres a year, which slipped through our fingers that day, and a whole drama, an unexpected, if not violent, death, a whole story, which I'll tell you one day . . . for it's now the time when I have to go to meet the one who wants to be another Barbara for me.

"We made a gift to that lady of the soul of Atala. All the collectors in Amsterdam were crammed into our sale; there were crazy bids, but we didn't sell Atala; it would have been tantamount to selling a fragment of our soul. We also saved a few jewels, souvenirs and miniatures, touching wreckage; you'll see them one evening in my home . . .

"The soul of Atala is in the lady's house. Conquered by our ideas, intoxicated by the glaucous and visionary charm that sleeps in bottles of conserves, that incomparable woman, to whose home I shall take you, possesses an entire museum today, Messieurs, a prestigious museum well made to please you. But I have to leave you; a woman can't be kept waiting!"

100

V
The Weepers' Tower

"A woman can't be kept waiting." That had been Monsieur de Bougrelon's adieu. By way of compensation, we were kept waiting for him, in vain, the next day and the two days that followed; Monsieur de Bougrelon did not reappear—and the rain was still falling, drowning in grayness and damp a monotonous city that had turned to mud and water: a land of phantoms in truth, of which the heroic friend of Monsieur de Mortimer was one of the illusory specimens, with his silhouette of a marionette, his jargon of the last century and the chimerical nature of his pretentions.

In any case, where could we find him? Monsieur de Bougrelon had completely neglected to give us his address—and that is a custom habitual to specters, of which the unreal gentleman certainly had the unexpected emergences from the shadows, and the abrupt disappearances.

All things considered, we had been dreaming. Our guide to the Netherlands had abandoned us as soon as we recovered our cool heads. Monsieur de Bougrelon was the product of our ennui, that foggy atmosphere and a few intoxications of schiedam; we had lent a body to our alcoholic dreams, a soul to the suggestions of paintings in museums, a voice to the melancholy of Prince Henry's Quay and the North Channel. And as the city, under the perpetual downpour, in spite of its glaring shop-fronts and the dives of the Ness, was becoming for us, with every passing hour, a city of spleen, we made the decision to leave Amsterdam. Oh, those three days of wandering, abandoned and dismal, through private collections, those centuries of hours spent, eyes stuck to magnifying-glasses, examining unknown masters and jewels in display-cases in the insipid atmosphere, reeking of pepper and wax polish, of collectors' galleries.

On the fourth morning, we could take no more. The rain, however, had called a truce, and the opaque fog that framed our windows was opalescent in places thanks to rays of sunlight. Even so, we buckled our suitcases, and, with my fingers clenched on a recalcitrant strap, I was holding the abnormal inflation of an overnight bag under the pressure of a knee, when the door of my room opened wide, and, preceded by a formidable "Bonjour! Oh, you're leaving, Messieurs!" his unexpected silhouette loomed up on my threshold. It was him; Monsieur de Bougrelon had returned to us.

It was him, but this time, even more fantastic and terrible, a sinister and macabre Monsieur de Bougrelon, for on that last morning, a broad black band cut the thinness of that spectral face in two. Livid, his long dyed moustache bristling more than ever, Monsieur de Bougrelon had a bandage over one eye. Monsieur de Bougrelon had come back to us half-blind.

One hand posed on the turquoise pommel of an enormous cane. Bougrelon was braced in a narrow olive-green frock-coat, and in a peremptory tone: "I nearly died, and by the hand of the graces. Yes, in truth, Messieurs, a woman's trinket nearly went into my eye—one of those golden needles with which the little women of Marken Island ornament their foreheads like as many antennae—you know, the little Salomes that are the delight of fishermen hereabouts.

"My noble friend, the Lady of Beauty, with whom I play a game of ombre every evening, has taken her into her service, and as that little Gotte has a pretty face and freshness, the other evening—the same evening when I quit you, Messieurs—there are such incomparable liqueurs in the house . . . as I was coming down the stairs, the girl preceding me and carrying a candle, I felt in a playful mood—a ridiculous thing at my age, but before anything else, one is French—and, taking the girl by the waist, I tried to rub my old ape's muzzle on her peach-like skin, and misfortune overtook me, Messieurs, for the surprised pullet turning round abruptly, dug her crest into my eye.

"Into the eye—or nearly! Into the temple it would have been sudden death, Messieurs, a just punishment for my clowning. Does one play Leander at my age!—thank God I'm only Horatius Cocles.[1] But admit it, Messieurs, this becomes my beauty. Inès de Castro was one-eyed and a King of Spain loved her;[2]

---

1 Leander is a stock character of the Italian *commedia dell'arte*, imported into France by Pierre Corneille and others; once a plausible lover, he was transformed over time into a comic figure whose compulsive amorous advances only stimulated revulsion and hilarity. Horatius Cocles, familiar in England as the hero of the most oft-quoted passage in Macaulay's *Lays of Ancient Rome*, lost an eye while holding the bridge single-handed against Rome's would-be invaders.

2 Inès de Castro (1325-1355) was the lover of King Pedro I of Portugal; her murder by his disapproving father unleashed a storm of bloody revenge and gave rise to a legendary account of the

I am, therefore, de Castro, and that consoles me, or, although a Norman, I'm related to the Toledan race by an ancestor—De Castro, not castrato: don't confuse the two, ha ha!

"But I've arrived just in time; you're about to depart, and I can shake your hands. You're taking the eleven o'clock train—another twenty minutes and I'd have missed you. I'd never have forgiven myself, Messieurs, for, thanks to you, in enabling you to visit the city, I've relived the Amsterdam of Monsieur de Mortimer. Frenchmen like you are a rare windfall in the dismal epoch in which I find myself behind the times. One only sees princes of the flea-market and traveling sales-men nowadays. You must have thought me dead, and I ought to have informed you, I know—but does one get annoyed with friends over such trivia? Oh, you're leaving; the fog of this country is not good for your health; only an exile can be content in Amsterdam. You're leaving, and perhaps we'll never see one another again."

And taking an enormous brass chronometer from his fob pocket, a sort of navigator's compass-watch, he said: "Ten to eleven; you've missed the train, Messieurs, and thanks to me—yes, I flatter myself and I applaud myself for it. It would have been hard for me to see you depart without having downed a few schiedams together. You won't refuse me the honor of sitting you down at my table today. I invite you to lunch; it's me who'll treat you this time."

---

coronation of her exhumed corpse, thus lending a valuable motif to subsequent generations of tragedians. The notion that she was missing an eye is, however, idiosyncratic.

And we had lunch, that morning, with Monsieur de Bougrelon; in accordance with his praiseworthy habit, he left it to us to settle the bill, but he had lost his customary loquacity and good humor; a visible anxiety was disturbing that indefatigable talker. Was it the malaise inherent in any departure? It was as if something between us had broken; an atmosphere of sadness and mistrust filled the little subterranean room in the Staawertstraat restaurant. After all, perhaps his recent accident had indisposed the old gentleman, for Monsieur de Bougrelon got up twice to go to the kitchen to refresh his compresses and bathe his eye; Gotte's gold pin was evidently causing him pain.

"In Avranches, in the times when Monsieur de Mortimer and I were unfortunate there, that scratch would have healed in an hour—an hour, what am I saying? in five minutes the flesh would have been bandaged, sown up, and the skin as smooth as a fruit. Monsieur de Mortimer possessed a marvelous ointment, Messieurs; I have, alas, mislaid the formula. That formula dated from the crusades, Messieurs; it had been brought back from the Orient, from Jerusalem itself, or rather from Persepolis, by a prince of the house of Bouillon, who died thereafter in the Holy Land, and the Mortimer family had it from a Princess of Cleves married into or descended from the said Bouillons.[1] A thousand various ingredients entered into it, hyssop, the hair of a bat, antimony, crushed emerald and essence of mummy, Messieurs, a veritable Egyptian phar-

---

1 Godfrey of Bouillon was one of the leaders of the First Crusade in 1096, and became the first ruler of the Kingdom of Jerusalem.

macopeia; but no matter, such as it was, that ointment was customary to Edgard, and miraculous in its effect. I'll give you an example.

"Every morning, when we were in Avranches, Monsieur de Mortimer had the habit—he was crazy about horses and dogs—of going down to the kennels, and then the stables to stroke the animals and, if there was any need, reprimand the grooms; and as he was a big child, entire loaves were thrown to the dogs of the pack and slices of melon offered to the stallions, sugar lumps eaten from the hand, pats on the withers for the mares and pinches of the nose for the colts.

"Now, during one of those tours of the stable, a big Hungarian horse, which Edgard thought was gelded, but which was as entire, Messieurs, as you or me, a great chestnut rogue, tickled in passing, turned on Edgard and bit him cruelly. It bit his face, Messieurs and like an apple. There was a hideous, abominable wound, the entire jaw laid open, a gaping wound into which the heroic beauty of that admirable cavalier would sink forever.

"Anyone else would have killed the horse—a horse can be slain by a pistol-shot like a man. Mortimer went back to his apartments, took a pot of his ointment, and rubbed it on his cheek—and that evening, he dined in town; for that evening, there was no longer any sign of it.

"That, Messieurs, is what the men and the unguents of our epoch were like; compare them, if you dare, with the inventions of your time."

That was the only rodomontade in which the ordinarily sparkling fantasy showed during that bleak lunch, but that display exhausted Monsieur de Bougrelon; he only resumed his declamatory speech and aristocratic phraseology on Prince Henry's Quay, almost at the extremity of the Y, in front of the Weepers' Tower,[1] which he absolutely insisted on taking us to see that day.

And when we arrived at that great mass of stone: "The Weepers' Tower, Messieurs—in French, we would have used the feminine form of the noun, for in France men do not know tears, or at least ought not to know them. Dolor is essentially female, but these brave Dutchmen do not see so far. Joris, Jan or Peters departed for Borneo, Sumatra, Java or America; the father of Peters, the brother of Jan and the grandfather of Joris accompanied them as far as the ship, and there, on the quay, hugging them in their big arms with big tears in their big eyes of big men, the tears of seals and the sobs of porpoises, tears that scarcely embellished the porcelain irises of all those old apes of old Delft as they were painted by Teniers and all the Van Ostades or *sans Ostades*[2] of this land of winds and windmills; but it was with those adieux, regrets and despair that the stones of that tower were cemented, Messieurs. The French tradi-

---

1 *Tour des pleurers* [Weepers' Tower] is a translation of *Schreierstoren*, the name of the tower that was once part of the Medieval city wall; that label is actually a corruption of its original name, but a legend was invented to justify it alleging that it was named for the women who wept thereabouts when their men set sail on hazardous journeys; Monsieur de Bougrelon's suggestion that in the Dutch version the weepers are men is a fantasy.

2 The implication of this wordplay is not easy to grasp, as there is no obvious French word that the hypothetical painters cited might be without, but "Ostades" was employed in Dutch as the name of a variety of English cloth employed for making jackets.

tion, aristocratic as it is, makes amorous women weep there; the Dutch, who are realists, made old men sob dolorously, and use the masculine form of weepers.

"I want to weep here in my turn today, a great deal for me and a little for you, Messieurs: it's here that my coquetry wants to make you its adieux.

"We shall never see one another again; no one comes back to Holland; the dream of it one takes away; the memories that it imposes are more beautiful than the reality. It's necessary not to look back. Personally, I'm an exile, a hallucinated old man cloistered in a vision that I don't want to touch. I'm like an urn, Messieurs, but one still warm with the heat of ashes. Those ashes are the visions of my past, the vision of France such as I knew her, such as I left her, a France devoid of railways, telegraphs and telephones, a France not yet dishonored by factories and parliaments. In this land of canals at least I shall never see bicycles or automobiles, or a thousand hideous and barbaric things that I cannot even imagine, since I'm ignorant of them, but whose name alone is painful to me. And then, Monsieur de Mortimer, or his specter, still fills this city; he marches by my side when I go along the canals, he speaks to me in a low voice when I wander at a slow pace, in the evenings, at dusk, in our dear museum. The portraits that we loved together have, for me, the smiles, gestures and gazes of old accomplices. For me, Amsterdam is populated with dear phantoms, Messieurs; that's why I want to die here."[1]

---

1 The tenth episode in *Le Journal*, "La Tour des pleurers," ended here; the final one was entitled "Dame de Beauté" [Lady of Beauty].

※

"No, Messieurs, I shall never see France again," Monsieur de Bougrelon emphasized, in a melancholy fashion.

He had folded his arms over his chest, and his eyes had become singularly distant and empty.

"Anyway, what would I do there? All those I loved there are dead; I'd no longer recognize anyone there, and, something even more dolorous, no one would any longer recognize me.

"An exile is always alone, but perhaps less so in the land of his exile than in his own country. The joys of return: that's what he must never attempt, after thirty or forty years of absence. Just think! If one found nothing but an empty house, that would only be a partial disaster; phantoms have strange preferences for old dwellings and dormant memories, and sleep there like funereal swallows, wings folded, between the beams of the ceilings. There would be the dream of finding the house uninhabited and the garden neglected, but one never has the luck of bumping into the rusty gate and the closed shutters when one returns. No, the gate is newly painted, the shutters open, the garden maintained, the paths raked and the flower-beds blooming with geraniums, Messieurs! Geraniums, where one had left columbines, blue aconites and the exquisite obsolete grace of hollyhocks; and in the house, there are strangers . . .

"Strangers; do you understand the insult of that word, Messieurs? Faces that one does not know, and who look at you, faces of mistrust and hostility, the abominable and bourgeois faces of proprietors.

The house is mine; it's for you to get out of it.

"No, I won't expose myself to that horrible welcome, that dagger-thrust in my old heart. At least here, in the distance and the absence, I can still see, as I left it, the old house in Avranches where I grew up; and it's my Childhood, and my dear Past of twenty-five years, which always seems to be waiting for me in my dreams, both huddled in the corner of the hearth, in the ashes, the former having become an old maidservant, a quavering and octogenarian grandmother, and the latter still as young and handsome as it was at fifteen, half a century ago, Messieurs, for only our childhood grows old in our memory; our past is protected from that by love; the age when one was loved blazes with such an intense aurora.

"But my two dear phantoms have not waited for me; the Bougrelon house was put up for sale a long time ago. Twenty years ago, it was the local tax office; paper-pushers were installed in it, ink-stained nuisances. It's probably a restaurant today. Can you see me disembarking, Messieurs, to find my venerated specters turning the spit or waiting on tables? Haven't I told you that I've lived in Holland for more than thirty years of my life as an exile; I ought to die here and I want to die here."

Monsieur de Bougrelon no longer had his habitual bombast; even his theatrical gestures had disappeared.

110

He spoke with his chest till stuck out, but his shoulders not thrust so far back, both hands leaning on the pommel of his cane, and his eagle-eyed stare had become vague, troubling us with its sadness. Monsieur de Bougrelon was talking almost like anyone else; he was an unknown de Bougrelon; a human being had emerged from the marionette; in that corseted individual, made up and stiffened in a determined attitude, there was, therefore, humanity, true sadness and dolor.

Before us was the bleak and sandy extent of the waters of the Zuiderzee, crested on the horizon by moving foam—for the wind was beginning to rise out to sea—a sky swept with russet clouds into which sudden fissures imported shreds of blue air, a true Dutch sky as painters paint it, a sky in which one evokes the sails of windmills or the yardarms of fishing-boats, with, far away to our right, the enormous round mass of the Weepers' Tower. Monsieur de Bougrelon had fallen silent and, our hearts somewhat constrained by the melancholy of those adieux, we respected his silence. We walked thus along the edge of Prince Henry's Quay for nearly ten minutes.

"But I don't want to keep you any longer, Messieurs," our guide put in, abruptly. "I made you miss the train this morning; once is sufficient. Go, yes, it's time; I'm beginning to like you, Messieurs, and tomorrow I'd suffer too much on seeing you leave. The heart of the old is like ivy; one becomes attached quickly when one is alone."

Almost immediately, though, he amended the judgment: "Alone no, I'm not that, since the mercy has been granted to my exile and my old age to have beside me the most noble and most delicate affection, for do I not have to retain me here the most solid bond, that devoted and vigilant creature who wants to be another Barbara to me, that Lady of Beauty whose admirable collection I promised to take you to visit some day, her collection of conserves: conserves, one of the unsuspected vestiges of this land of visions!

"Yes, I remember, I made you that promise; I said that I would take you there, and then other occupations claimed us. Can one do as one wishes? Then again, I was too enthusiastic in describing those conserves to you; that visit might perhaps have disappointed you, and, I confess, I would not have forgiven you for that disappointment. You have lent your souls to my divagations, to the dreams of a hallucinated old man, and I am infinitely grateful to you for having allowed me to cultivate in you the phantasms of my dreams

"It's like the petty lodgings I inhabit, of which I wanted to do you the honors; just room to turn around, messieurs, a true half-pay officer's roost, but I have a few curious bibelots there, priceless to me: a miniature of Barbara, one of Mercedes with her ruby frame, and a few jewels, relics of a more fortunate epoch. All of that I would have shown you, but time was lacking, my determination was turned to the wind of other caprices; and then, trinkets of that sort only have value to their possessor.

112

"A portrait is always a treason; the only worthwhile ones are those of unknown individuals. And then, what would you have thought of me if you had visited my hovel? A hovel, yes, Messieurs, it would be a hovel in France; but with the meticulous neatness of these Dutch folk, it's an attic. What would you have thought, on seeing a Bougrelon thus lodged? I'm poor, what do you expect? No, you wouldn't have thought anything, for I know the delicacy of your souls; better than that, you will never think or believe anything bad of me, Messieurs, although someone might relate some slander to you one day about the name de Bougrelon that will suggest it. That I know."

And, abruptly putting his cane under his arm, in order to take our hands, and while he was holding them affectionately clasped in his: "Of that attic of a fallen gentleman, that monkish cell, Messieurs, I would, however, have done you the honors, if I had had a portrait there to show you of my friend de Mortimer.

"My friend de Mortimer! That man, I have talked about so much that you almost know him, and I would have liked to engrave in your memory the indelible features of that heroic and charming face; but I did not even have that motive any more. I had more than ten portraits of Edgard; I burned them all; none of them resembled him.

"Adieu, Messieurs."

And, with an unexpected pirouette, he turned on his heels and disappeared, as if he had fallen into the canal.

We should not have seen Monsieur de Bougrelon again. A person of mystery, he should have taken the enigma of his life with him and left us the alarming obsession. That would have been the esthetic perfection of this story; unfortunately, there is only esthetic perfection in the adventures I have invented, and Monsieur de Bougrelon is not a character of invention.

We saw him again the same evening, and in the most fortuitous of circumstances, the most unexpected and the simplest. On the very evening of that solemn adieu, hazard, which had brought that hallucinatory silhouette out of the shadows for us, was to snatch away the mask of the phantom and destroy the scaffolding, so laboriously elevated, of so many heroic pretentions.

It was written that we would miss the train twice that day. On returning to the hotel there was an encounter with a friend from Paris who had arrived at midday, while we were lunching elsewhere, and who was lying in wait for us at the Adrian. A glance at the register had informed him of our presence at the hotel, and that dear Pointel, delighted with the stroke of luck, had no intention of letting us leave.

"Pure chance, but of which I'm taking advantage," he declared to us on taking possession of us in the lobby. "I'm not letting you go again. It's the first time I've been in Amsterdam; you've been here a week, informed and documented on the museums and the walks, and I'll let you go? No, not so stupid."

And as we objected—our bags packed, our return tickets!—he went on: "Bah! You'll grant me the evening. You'll have all the time until midnight to inform me. It's settled; we'll dine together—I'm inviting you. This evening you can take me to see the splendors of the Ness, where I've already nosed around at dusk."

Awkward, in fact! One cannot refuse a compatriot in distress one's guidance, just for one evening, in the legendary Venusberg of Amsterdam. We therefore accepted Pointel's invitation. Having drunk the coffee, we took him to the Ness.

It was not to the Ness that we went, however, but to the Seadeck, the district of sailors and dives, something like the old port quarter of Marseille and the old Rydeck of Antwerp, a distant suburb situated behind the solitudes of the station, reserved for the frolics of cosmopolitan mariners and the basest prostitution. The place is rather dangerous; the drunkenness of sailors, when it is aggravated by lust, easily brings knives into play, and the canal is such a convenience for getting rid of embarrassing cadavers in the foggy Netherlands. But the Seadeck is the district of taverns, dance-halls and cafés with live music; there is love of all kinds there, and songs in all languages; the Seadeck is the great dancing, singing and fornicating truancy of the Netherlands; we had the strength of numbers and, flanked by an interpreter, we went to the Seadeck.

We had already visited five or six dives when, in one of those cabarets of matelots where there was dancing, an establishment that was simultaneously a bar and a ballroom, in the red and thick atmosphere of those sorts of places, misted with breath, smoky with tobacco, with the bitter smell of sweat and alcohol, salt and tar, everything floating in one of those oily gleams dear to the brush of Rembrandt, what did we see? Sitting on the stage reserved for the orchestra, dominating with his bow the wooly heads of negro mariners and the caps of America sailors in the process of dancing a joyful polka, what did we see?

Phantasmal and rigid, pinched in his olive-green frock-coat with his black bandage over his eye, Monsieur de Bougrelon!

Impassive and livid, his chin leaning on his violin, Monsieur de Bougrelon was making the clientele in reefer jackets and cheap boots dance; around him, turning heavily two by two, hands on shoulders, was the cheerful prancing crowd of polka-dancers. Monsieur de Bougrelon, with his profile of an old wounded eagle, under his black bandaged forehead, surpassed them all in height, like a statue of Orpheus: a macabre Orpheus accompanied by a Eurydice in tartan, pitiful and faded; for an aged female harpist, a lamentable carcass of a grandmother in an immense Pamela hat and an old discolored checkered shawl draped over a poor silk dress that had once been green, was sitting next to Monsieur de Bougrelon. An antique Empire harp was weeping sadly under her mitten-gloved hands, while along the violin his hand, his fleshless hand, with feverish and frantic fingers, clutched and ran convulsively, like a crab.

And we understood where the old gentleman spent all his evenings. We possessed the key to the enigma; we knew why our dear and aged guide left us so pre-

116

cipitately every evening; we knew, and with what sadness, what game of ombre—and it was not of shadows but of specters that it was necessary to speak[1]—the old gentleman played with the lady of the nobility who wished him well.

What! That was the Lady of Beauty, the lady with the private chapel where he attended mass and vespers every Sunday, the lady with the museum of conserves, the other Barbara, and so on?

Monsieur de Bougrelon had lied, impudently, about Monsieur de Mortimer, and that heroic and sumptuous youth, and so many duels, so many adventures, and that exile, and that black bandage over his eye—in such milieux, surely sustained in a scuffle or brawl . . .

Monsieur de Bougrelon was a musician in a sailors' dive.

We were dumbstruck with stupor in the entrance to the ballroom. Monsieur de Bougrelon had raised his head and had just perceived us; not a muscle quivered in his wan and tragic face; he continued playing as if nothing had happened—except that his remaining eye was closed; he had lowered the eyelid.

Monsieur de Bougrelon did not want to see us.

Respectful of his desire, we left without recognizing him.

---

1 This wordplay works slightly better in English than in French, because the card-game whose name is rendered *ombre* [shadow] in English is rendered as *hombre* in French, reflecting the implication of its original Spanish version.

EPILOGUE
TO *MONSIEUR DE BOUGRELON*

He has appeared to me. Yes, him—the man who was the enchantment, and, slightly, the regret, of my brief sojourn in the land of canals and windmills. The man whose phantasmal silhouette, prestigious verbiage and epic bombast animated and populated the fogs of Amsterdam for me, and the North Sea; the man of castles in Spain, evoked by a word and a gesture—but what a word of genius and what a superb gesture, in the mist and rain of the Netherlands!

The man who gave speech to the portraits in the museum, the gallant costumes of vanished centuries, and even the soul of bottles of conserves; yes, the magician of the Seadeck, of old frames and display-cases, Monsieur de Bougrelon came, at a distance of exactly a year, to reveal himself to me in the heart of Provence—but a rainswept and dismal Provence, a Provence spoiled by downpours, thus having become even sadder, without the sun, than the sandy dunes of the sad Netherlands—and in rather singular circumstances.

There were three manifestations.

The first occurred in Marseille, a Marseille still streaming with the inundation of that first of January 1898, but already warmed again by two mornings of lovely sunshine.

It was on the Monday, the third of that month, in truth, toward noon, at the hour when the Cannebière wriggles and swarms with the incessant comings and goings of its cosmopolitan crowd, going up and down the celebrated lanes to the masts of the Old Harbor. On the Quai de la Fraternité, there were the usual troops of street-porters sampling scallops and sea-urchins from the stalls of shellfish-merchants, pell-mell with the fat merchants of the city—because that is also the hour when the Bourse is going full tilt. The sun-trap of the Cheminée du Roi René, between the Place Victor-Gelu and the church of Saint-Augutin, was enlivened by the chatter and gaiety of dock-workers and stevedores returning from La Joliette.

Oh, the odors of garlic and bouillabaisse!

Intoxicated by the crowd, whose anonymity delighted me, I allowed myself to be drawn by it to a booth where idlers had formed a circle.

A group of shoeshine boys and fishwives was gesticulating there, with whores from La Tourette, flirting with tobacco-chewers, all roguish, with shiny dark eyes and thick lips drawn back over white teeth, all curiously leaning over two lamentable burnooses fallen on the sidewalk: two old Arabs in hoods, heaps of verminous rags and extenuated flesh, fallen there exhausted, under the feet of the pedestrians.

Long waxy faces with long white beards and extinct gazes, the faces of millenarian prophets, the two Arabs remained motionless under the inquisitive, indifferent gazes, as if they were on the parvis of their mosque, and their mummified hands continued, mechanically, to knead the yellow and wrinkled soles of their bare feet. Both had disembarked that morning, no doubt— Monday is one of the days when ferries arrive from Tunis and Algiers. In front of them, there were the masts of the Old Harbor and the blue of the deceptive sea. With their profiles of old dromedaries, as they reeked of plague and the Orient, the spices of soukhs and palm-wine, the two pitiful wrecks of Algeria lay there in the soil of exile.

"From Mecca to the m**de!"[1]

And the thunderous voice, which summarized the situation so well, risked the last final gamble. Insulting as the remark was for the port of Marseille, the definition of the exodus of those poor Berbers was so powerful in its unexpected sound that I could not retain a smile. I turned round to salute the author of the bold remark with a wink, but there were only Marseillais there; I had therefore been dreaming, unless I had been thinking aloud.

"From Mecca to the m**de!" That was not my language. Where had I heard that imperious, bombastic voice, the timbre of those emphatic syllables?

Only Monsieur de Bourgrelon would have had that audacity in the comparison, that unexpectedness in the ellipse, he alone that tone of a commandant giving the order to open fire—but I confess, to my shame, that I did not think of him for a minute, and, without lingering any further in vain reflections, I went back to

---

1 In France, *merde* [shit] was considered too obscene to be reproduced in print in 1898 or 1935. Much of the scandal caused by *Ubu roi* resulted from the fact that the protagonist's first act is to bawl "Merdre!" at the audience, the precautionary extra letter failing to disguise the obscenity. Whereas *merde* is a stronger expletive in France than its English equivalent, *bougre* is a weaker one than the English "bugger," having largely, but not entirely, lost the implication of sodomy.

the hotel to pack my bags, because I was leaving that evening for Toulon.

Toulon, its flat bay, a silken blue under a hot sky at the foot of its burning mountains; the coming and going of its boatmen chatting barefoot on the quay of the old harbor with the white flapping of sails, its open circle of wooded hills, Saint-Mandrier and Tamaris, and between the tall chimerical factory silhouettes of its warships, the flash and surge of launches and the double splash of oars, scintillating with water and sunlight: the Toulon of May, the Toulon of June, the Toulon, the Touon of joy, the Toulon of the Mocotie in rut and Provence of idleness, that I could not rediscover!

Cities of the Midi, all of whose charm is in the light, and whose mirage is all of your beauty, it is necessary never to see you in winter! No, it isn't cheerful, Toulon in the rain. Gray and harsh mountains beneath a vaporous sky, muddy and stinking streets, in which the amber tint of Provençal womanhood becomes, in the damp shade, a suspect pallor, and all those carefree and broad-backed Moco fellows, rutilant with health in the semi-nakedness of warm seasons, become so pitiful once wrapped up in winter clothing, with the dirty appearance of their complexion and the awkwardness of their gestures in the reefer jackets and woolen pullovers of the Northern laborer.

Heartbroken not to have rediscovered, under the leafless plane-trees of the pathways, either the luminous heaps of yellow carnations of the June markets, nor their tender bunches of pink carnations, so delicately flavored with vanilla, nor the moist flesh of beautiful and riotous red carnations—oh, those poor anemic little roses and ill-advised mimosas supposedly sent from Nice!—I had resumed the road to the merchant port in the pouring rain.

There, before a misty horizon, I evoked the green-gold, pink-gold and turquoise-gold dusk in which, amid the odors of sweat and tar, pomade and oranges, I collected, on a certain evening of the previous summer, delicious jargon from the mouth of a Toulonnaise in a flowery cotton camisole: a beautiful girl! Surely, so brown was she and so well set in her primitive and supple beauty, she was the issue of a long line of Mocote fisher-folk. Her two hands posed on the shoulders of a sailor, the amorous Mocote had twittered these words:

"Come into the pine-woods; we'll be much cooler there to caress one another—but don't open your eyes too wide; you're frightening me."

A hectic flight of black waxed reefer-jackets, a raucous appeal to a distant tram, bound for Le Mourillon, and two sailors splashing through the muddy puddles, backs rounded, under the same umbrella—that's the dusks of Toulon in winter.

And the same voice that had spoken to me in Marseille pronounced these words in my ear:

"To have come back—what imprudence!"

Having turned around, I did not see anyone there, any more than I had on the quay of the Old Harbor.

I was being tracked by a shade; an invisible presence was accompanying me; a frightful experience was speaking for me.

With the taste for debauchery that sadness and ennui imparts to us, I made my way slowly to the red light district, the famous Chapeau-Rouge, where Toulonnais officialdom has the pretention of confining prostitution: the Chapeau-Rouge, as renowned in the annals of the navy as the Reboul district in Marseille and the old Rydeck in Antwerp.

In the midst of the flow of reefer jackets and berets, in a glare of light, the Cristal-Bar was once resplendent. All mirrors and marble, it was a large hall broadly open to the street, whose luxury insulted the cotton peignoirs and andrinople dresses of the whores in the houses opposite. There was dancing in that bar; waltz tunes and polkas emerged, molded by an old player piano, whose handle was turned by a volunteer sailor. And sailors and marines, the high blue collars of State uniforms and white helmets of the marine infantry, jostled one another, whirling and prancing pell-mell with the mocos and boatmen of the port.

Men reigned there as masters, because the Cristal-Bar was forbidden to women; a girl introduced into the midst of all those virilities would inevitably have given rise to brawls. Under the benevolent eye of the police, my brother Yves[1] and Marius, all the friends of the watch, Baptistin and Tann, all the encounters of the tropics, waltzed there, hands on shoulders, entirely given over to the physical pleasure of the dance, jeal-

---

1 This reference is evidently to the unruly Breton sailor in *Mon Frère Yves* (1883), a quasi-autobiographical novel by Pierre Loti; the other names cited are more difficult to pin down, but Baptistin might refer to the crooked valet featured in *Le Comte de Monte Cristo*.

ously watched, from the other side of the street, by the penciled eyes of the women.

I rediscovered the Chapeau-Rouge in unison with the city, de-souled and dismal: a wintry Chapeau-Rouge, its side-streets almost deserted; here and there, the silhouette of a sailor run aground in the hall of a dive, a sad whore sitting at the table with him, pouring him a drink; no more oaths, no more joyful jeers but, in equivocal cul-de-sacs, hurried muffled footfalls of muddy espadrilles, conversations in low voices between men with the appearance of pimps—and finally, in the middle of the street, a black patch, blacker than the night; shutters set over the entire façade of the Cristal-Bar, with a piece of paper stuck to the door bearing the simple words: *Closed because of change of ownership.*

Closed! The Cristal-Bar was closed! Why had I come back?

A hooded form that I had not noticed at first, leaning on the frontage, a species of man enveloped up to the eyes in a long black reefer-jacket, took a step toward me and in a voice already heard:

"To have had the good fortune to be able to love a locale, to have known the joy of living and letting live there, to have had the vertigo of a sensation to the extent of transmitting the frisson to others, and to have dared to come back, to have hoped to resuscitate something dead, without thinking for a moment that the irreparable march of time makes dust and nothingness of everything we have loved, that the past is a charnel-house, and that, outside of our hearts, everything down here is a sepulcher . . . !"

Like all specters, the man had no face, but I had recognized him. It was *him*! He alone, the poor musician of the sailors' dives of Amsterdam, could have been evoked on the threshold of that naval mariner-trap.

"But a memory, Monsieur . . . one cloisters oneself in a memory, walling oneself up in an extinct happiness, like a monk in a cell! But a memory, Monsieur, that is respected, when one has one, and the memory you had of this place—what a luminous *in pace* for a soul! What use has my example been to you, me, who never wanted to see France again for fear of not finding it as I had left it, me, who spent thirty years of my life wandering in exile in the company of a specter? It's necessary to die in Toulon, Monsieur, never to leave it, or never to see it again. If I had abandoned Amsterdam for a single day, do you think I would have rediscovered Monsieur de Mortimer there?"

The man without a face had vanished.

I shivered, thinking about the soul that had spoken to me, at a distance of a year, from Holland to Provence, from Amsterdam to Toulon.

A mouth of shadow had translated my thoughts aloud.

And I understood that Monsieur de Bougrelon was dead.

BABAUD MONIER'S CAT

WHEN it was learned that Babaud Monier's cat had talked there was a great emotion in the spinner's quarter, where the old woman lived. Babaud lived at the entrance to the wood of the Hanged Man, set back a little way from the main road in an old abandoned courtyard, a former cider-apple orchard returned to the wild state, which was known as the Clos Muré.

Yes, Babaud's cat could talk, just like a human.

Mère Ledun, the mattress-maker, had distinctly heard it say, in a strange voice: "Rain will fall this evening." She and Babaud were chatting, sitting on Monier's doorstep, with the door wide open, as it was the end of May. One o'clock had just chimed; the old spinster had just cleared the table of the remains of her meal. Suddenly, from the back of the kitchen, a bizarre, slightly nasal voice rose up, and in the silence of the room, the voice—which one might have thought that of a hunchback, a dwarf or a farfadet—pronounced the phrase clearly: "Rain will fall this evening."

The two women were stupefied by it. They looked at one another, their hearts slightly constricted; the same idea cut off their breath. There was surely someone hiding in the grain-loft: some practical joker who wanted to give them a scare. Someone was playing a trick on them.

After a brief silence, La Monier shook her chin. It was impossible, since she had taken down the ladder to the loft the previous evening.

Nor was it some practical joker lingering on the road. The Clos Muré was a long way back from the départemental highway, and in any case, they would have seen him go by; the Clos Muré is on a slope, it climbs the hill where the tall trees of the Hanged Man commence, and Babaud's house was backed up to a corner of the wall, like an old swallow's nest. The strange prediction did not come from the road, nor from the grain-loft.

Then the mysterious voice had suddenly continued, in the silence: "Rain will fall this evening, the meadows are green, the sky is dark."

This time, Babaud and La Ledun were so shocked that, with the same gesture, they each dropped the cup of coffee that they were sipping in the pleasant sunlight.

Having advanced her head, La Ledun had perceived, in the kitchen, La Monier's cat Mirou, which, sitting between two andirons in the ashes of the fire, was looking at them with an odd expression. His large green eyes had seemed enormous and flamboyant, like the bottles of the pharmacist in the main street, and Mirou seemed to have grown himself,

That had happened rapidly, in the penumbra of the kitchen, with the shutters closed, but Babad had had the same thought.

"I think your cat, Mamzelle Monier, has a peculiar physiognomy; where did you get that animal?"

"It's a cat found in a doorway, which I don't like either. It's solitary, and doesn't have anything to do with the other cats. It's cold to stroking, and nourishes itself on air; it doesn't hunt mice, or other animals. It isn't even amorous in the season. As funny things go, it's a funny cat."

"If I were you, Mamzelle Monier, I wouldn't care to have that animal in my house. There's something about it I don't like."

"What do you expect, it's a habit. It keeps me company—and then, Mirou doesn't cost me anything. But I don't like it much, for it doesn't say anything to me, either."

"Ah! You think that it doesn't say anything?"

Babaud shivered nervously; the two women had understood one another.

"You think it's him, then?" asked the old woman, her voice slightly strangled.

"My opinion is that it can only be him."

"Oh, the dirty beast! If I were sure I'd throw him out!"

Now, Mirou, with the marvelous instinct of his species, having divined that he was no longer safe in the house, had prudently slipped away. With velvet steps he had gone outside and he was now curled up, asleep, in an apple tree, at the fork of two branches, the bark of which his claws were kneading joyfully.

And it was thus that the legend was established throughout the region that Babaud Monier's cat could talk.

Babaud Monier, a virtuous spinster, had spent forty years of her life in service in the home of Madame de Chamarande, who had left her a small income and the enjoyment of the Clos Muré. Babaud Monier had been a model maidservant, honest and sober, with mores above suspicion. She lived on an annuity of six hundred francs from her former mistress and a few flowers that she cultivated with difficulty in the stony ground of her orchard.

La Monier scared me a little. She lived, it seemed to me, so far from the town; then again, the high wood of the Hanged Man, with its sinister name, impressed me, and the name of the Clos Muré did not leave me indifferent.

That old abandoned enclosure, the high walls that surrounded it, and the confusion of big creviced trees with twisted, branched trunks, some of them clad with gray moss, as if bearded, the majority supported by stakes, aged apple trees on crutches, evoking the idea of paralytic trees, all penetrated me with a mysterious terror. The beautiful flowers that Babaud cultivated had the effect on me of a fay's garden; a strange illumination, harsher than anywhere else, it seemed to me then, made all those flowers flamboyant. I thought involuntarily of the garden of the fay Gerbote, the story of which always haunted me on entering the Clos Muré:

She lived in a building with a thatched roof, set at the bottom of a large bank planted with beeches; twenty-five sorcerers changed by her into trees for ancient misdeeds were convulsed within the bark of twenty-five apple trees. That orchard of justice was guarded by flowers.[1]

In my childish imagination, I confounded Babaud Monier with the fay Gerbote. The sinister old woman had a nutcracker profile, a mouth with thin lips, toothless and caved in, and a bulbous nose covered in blackheads.

And then, that old little dwelling wedged in the angle between two walls, collapsing, as if from fatigue, run aground there like someone who can do no more, also had a maleficent appearance, as did Babaud Monier's garden, acceded by five steps—five shaky and mossy steps on which the old spinster sat, like a spider in its web amid the tangle of the branches of the apple trees.

So, when I learned, along with the entire town, that Mirou, Babaud Monier's cat, had talked, I was not particularly alarmed by the news; I was even astonished that the usage of speech had not been discovered in Mirou previously: that sorcerer cat was well-adapted to the frame of Babaud and her orchard. During my visit to the Clos with my grandmother, a giant ostrich could have come, as in the tales of Hoffmann, to greet us on the threshold and introduce us with a reverence into the old woman's hovel, and I would not have been greatly surprised; tales impassioned me then and I lived, a partly-awakened sleeper, in a kind of fantastic atmosphere.

---

1 This is not a reference to a real *conte de fées*, although the idea of a fay who transmutes her infidel lovers into trees recalls "Le Palais de vengéance" (tr. as "The Palace of Vengeance") by the Comtesse de Murat, in which the fay Ceore inflicts that punishment.

And Mirou continued to provide his own: his oracles on rain and good weather supplied topics of conversation to the whole region. He was a large yellow cat with magnificent eyes, two emeralds carved in the shape of almonds, simultaneously indolent and wild, which gazed at people from above and he did not disturb himself for anyone in a corner that he had adopted. He seemed to disdain visits, spoke at his whim, in the presence or in the absence of the curious and sometimes, in the midst of a fine assembly, got up from his place, and with his tail aloft, leaving the visitors standing there, went at a majestic pace to the gate.

His malice was diabolical. One day, the deputy maire, Monsieur Rabue, who was interested in metempsychosis and believed in the souls of animals, was curious to see the animal and came to the Clos Muré. Mirou was then perched on the summit of the wall, where he was purring at the sun; neither Babauid's pleas nor her joined hands, nor her threats, nor the presence of Monsieur Rabue had been able to persuade Mirou to come down . . . and yet, his vogue was augmented.

Freemasons and freethinkers could laugh and jeer as much as they wanted; pilgrimages to the Clos Muré were hastened. Society ladies had learned the way to the Clos; one found oneself in choice company there now, the time of Mère Ledun, the mattress-maker and the local menders was long gone; children were brought there as to puppet shows; Babaud had doubled the price of her flowers.

La Monier could have made a lot of money if Mirou had consented to talk at the injunctions of his mistress, but he was an eccentric beast who only operated at his own times. There were weeks when Mirou remained silent for entire days, and others when he rambled on like a drunken parrot. *Rain will fall this evening, the meadows are green, the sky is dark. The mole is in the fields, the ears of wheat inclining. It's necessary to sow by moonlight. Love at Candlemas the rose and the snow in flower*: aphorisms and obscure doggerel added to Mirou's prestige. Mirou spoke in the language of the gods and almanac verses.

One strange thing completed impressing and convincing people: Mirou never opened his mouth when he enunciated mysterious statements regarding the wheat, the mole and the snow in flower; his jaws remained motionless; Mirou retained his pretty, enigmatic and disquieting face of a sacred animal. His voice floated from the kitchen, coming, one might have thought, from on high, nested in the hollows of the beams, between the sheaves of corn, the blocks of lard and the chaplets of onions. Mirou was a ventriloquist. Worse, or better, he had days when he made himself invisible; the voice spoke when Mirou was not there! Babaud Monier lived penetrated by respect, gratitude and fear.

"Have you dined well, Babaud?"

That day, it was too much. When the old spinster heard her cat address her as *tu*, she caught a fever and was bedridden. The neighbors, anxious at not seeing her tending her flowers in the Clos, found her shivering, sweating and paralyzed. Her three old teeth were clicking with terror.

"It *tutoyed* me! It *tutoyed* me! It called me by my name; I'm going to die."

"Have you dined well, Babaud?" sniggered the voice.

The neighbors made the sign of the cross; there was even more devilry than usual; La Ledun talked about drowning the accursed animal. A coincidence determined that Mirou disappeared the same day. He was not seen again. Weary of so many visits, disgusted by so much stupidity and sated with success, perhaps he had departed for the hospitable thickets of the Hanged Man, delighted to return to the wild state after having seen at close range the unhealthy ineptitude of humans— Mirou was a peaceful cat—or perhaps, warned by his animal instinct of the evil projects being ripened in his regard, he had prudently sought another abode.

His departure was deplored, but that flight, as mysterious as the rest, did not save the invalid. Mirou might have vanished but his magnificent soul remained in the Clos, and in the beams of the ceiling the insidious voice continued to sneer: "Have you dined well, Babaud? Rain will fall this evening." Poor Monier, obstinate in thinking that someone had cast a spell on her, gasped and became delirious, appealing for aid to Jesus, the Virgin, Saint Ambroise and Saint Pancras. Her condition became so grave that even the pharmacist ceased joking and uttering his customary snigger: "That Babaud Monier . . . it's only old spinsters whose cats talk!"

It was then that the situation was aggravated by a strange circumstance, which proved the extent to which there was sorcery in it. Babaud had been in bed for a fortnight, agitated and feverish; Mère Ledun, the mattress-maker, and Lisa Henriot, the spinner, were watching over her.

One morning in August, at about four o'clock, Lisa Henriot heard a kind of noise above her head, a soft sound of limping feet: someone walking in the grain-loft. She nudged La Ledun, who was dozing beside her, and having consulted one another, the two women decided to go and see.

The ladder was applied to the trap-door. Lisa, the braver of the two, went up. Something fluttering and half-crawling tried to flee as she approached; it limped and it hopped; it was something black and formless, which gleamed in places as though it were phosphorescent; it took refuge in the straw. Two yellow eyes looked at Lisa, and in the gloomy grain-loft the hesitant Henriot put out a hand; a formidable beak-thrust dug into her thumb, a clatter of wings slapped her cheek, and, more dead than alive, she tumbled down the ladder, her agonized hand bloody.

"Jesus Maria, what is it?"

"*It* is a frightful beast in the grain loft, something that bites and pinches, and whose eyes shine like embers; for me, that's the reason poor Monier is dying; it's an ensorcelled beast, it limps and flutters like an owl."

"That's possible! It's seen to you, the beast!"

"For me, that's what jabbers and says nasty things to annoy everyone. Perhaps it's Mirou's soul?"

At six o'clock the neighbors were informed. Malroux, the blacksmith and a farmhand took it upon themselves to go up into the loft.

They were heard giving chase to the beast. They came back down holding by the wings a kind of owl, mewling and bloody: a big bird that one might have thought roasted by flames and blackened by soot, some animal burned by a fire or escaped from Hell. It opened a large black beak from which a heavy gray tongue hung down, and it darted large yellow eyes while uttering plaintive cries. Under the abdomen, when the feathers parted, the beast seemed bright blue and pink, and the undersides of its wings faded to pale yellow.

The women thought they would faint: "It's that damned Mirou, who's changed into an owl! He's cast a spell on his poor mistress!"

As it is befitting to punish sorcerers, and as popular resentment does not admit the inexplicable, the beast's neck was wrung, and then it was nailed to the door of the dwelling, two nails in the wings and one in the heart—which did not prevent Babaud Monier from dying the following night, still hearing her cat Mirou addressing her as *tu* and calling her by her name.

MADAME GERMONT'S PARROT

BABAUD MONIER had been dead for three months and the old woman's house was locked. No one had cared to take Babaud's succession. A house in which cats talk like natural people and suddenly change into birds is suspect in every country in the world, and most particularly in Normandy, where superstition has not yet said its final word.

The Clos Muré thus returned gaily to the wild state. The old apple trees buckled under the weight of their fruits, which had become bitter; the local brats disdained to maraud them. Through the coaching entrance, open to all comers, the old abandoned enclosure could be seen invaded by wild plants, from which burst forth, here and there, a ragged rose, hollyhocks or the orange-tinted crimson of large lilies, which had become even rarer. Gradually, the weeds stifled them.

Rich in corollas, butterflies, long grass and light, the enclosure of the Clos appeared an enchanted place, but no one went in there. The Clos was guarded by a bad memory, and also by an equivocal presence: the de-plumed wings of the evil beast nailed by the blacksmith

Malroux to the door, a kind of black-tinted bird with phosphorescent down, in which the old women had wanted to find the soul of Mirou, the sorcerer cat.

For three months the frightful beast had been rotting there under the sun and the rain, with a nail through its body and two others planted in its wings, and gradually, the filthy carrion dried out and flattened, stinking and lamentable. Its pitiful little skeleton now appeared beneath the split skin, vaguely agitated by swarming worms, its sad beak filled with clotted blood, and its image haunted the slumber of the old women of Moreux.

Sometimes, a boy going past the wide gate threw a pebble at the phantom bird, and all the resentment of the town was relieved by that cast stone. Old Babaud herself was asleep in the cemetery, in the common grave, as befit a poor maidservant who had lived in humility for seventy years.

Now it happened that one day in mid-November, Aldric Gromare, Madame Germont's farmer in the commune of Nointot-les-Fossés, was coming back from the Moreux market. He was heading for the road to Dieppe and was cutting through the spinner's quarter, known as the Queue-de-Renard. He went past the Clos Muré and, at the open coaching entrance, his peasant's avarice was stirred by the mess of apples rotting in pure waste; his instinct as a cultivator was indignant at all those apple-trees that had not been beaten. He went in, in order to evaluate the money squandered by an "idler" of a tenant, tasted an apple, pulled a face, and suddenly spotted the skeleton of the crucified bird.

"Eh? What's that? There's an owl that doesn't resemble others of its species."

As Aldric Gromare was inquisitive and cantankerous by nature, he climbed the five steps of Babaud's staircase and came to inspect the object at close range.

"Eh! Good God, it's Aramin, our old lady's parrot! She's been looking for it for a long time. Madame Germont's parrot, crucified like a screech-owl at the door of this hovel in an orchard of poisoned apples, what a misfortune! If she knew that, she'd be sure to fall ill; she loved Aramin so much, and it was sugared wine, biscuits, ripe figs in the season and grape pips that it pecked from her mouth, almost like a lover, and I'm scandalized to see her Aramin rotting there like a beast—such a well-cared-for animal, so pampered that she kicked up a fuss in three communes. Oh, for sure, if she learned what has become of her parrot, she'd start a lawsuit against the town; she isn't a woman to let go, and she has the means; but it isn't me whose going to tell her. She's also a woman who'd throw me and the children out and take the farm off us; it's not me, for sure, who'll break our mistress's heart. Those who've crucified her parrot like Our Lord, brigands of brigands, must be evil folk. Poor Aramin, what could you have said, to be rotting like a mole at the door of a barn, you who were more pampered among us than the nephew of a king? I'd like to know how it happened."

Retracing his steps, the peasant went down toward the spinners; he hesitated between the blacksmith's forge and the wig-maker's shop, and then decided on the tavern.

The Madame Germont whose parrot the farmer had just recognized was the chatelaine of Nointot-les-Fossés. She lived there for eight months of the year, in a kind of large two-story cabin flanked by a tower with a pointed roof, which had nothing seigneurial about it but its park. The house, a veritable barracks with its façade of twenty windows, dated from the worst of Louis-Philippe. The tower, felted with ivy and wisteria, was a former dovecot. Its mullioned windows and ancient moats permitted the dwelling to be given the name of château. The park commanded five farms and gave a good return. Madame Germont collected its usufruct.

She was a woman of sixty, well-conserved, who must have been beautiful; her attire remained youthful. She was very proud of her feet and her arms, which were very pale. She had been married; the society of the town never saw her. It was said that she had been in the theater; her appearance did not belie that opinion. Madame Germont remained very coquettish; she put into her toilette a studied luxury that the province did not admit. She dressed herself in Rouen; that circumstance did not make work for the seamstress of the town, and indisposed other women. It also discontented the suppliers.

Nevertheless, Madame Germont alone spent more than the mairesse and two notaries' wives, for, fond of frills and jewelry, always in quest of a bow, a ribbon, a flower for a hat, with a chain or a ring in need of repair or a piece of cloth to match, her coupé was frequently seen on the road from Nointot to the town, and Madame

Germont's horses—she harnessed them in pairs—were always stationed outside the shop of Madame Clara Muguet, milliner, Ernard the silversmith's, or the patisserie. Madame Germont was greedy.

All her faults, shown without any hypocrisy, completed compromising her in the minds of right-thinking people; however, Madame Germont did not appear to be troubled by an opinion that her marriage had alienated.

When Monsieur Germont, an old bachelor, a sexagenarian whose heritage was monitored by three married nephews established in the area, brought back that beautiful young woman scarcely thirty years old and installed her at Nointot there was a general outcry throughout the region. She had to be an adventuress who had got the old man to marry her; the age difference between them condemned the young woman in advance; she was only obedient to interest. The surrounding area, labored by Monsieur Germont's nephews and their wives' families, decided that no one would see the newcomer; her marriage already had the province up in arms, her appearance and her youth completed the indignation of consciences.

Madame Germont was pretty and elegant; her original attire deviated from received ideas. Old Monsieur Germont, very smitten, loved to see her adorned. To the jewels in her wedding-basket he added others. Madame Germont spent without counting. It requires no more, in Normandy, to depreciate a woman. No one rendered wedding visits to the château. Worse than that, Madame Germont had a bathroom installed in the old dovecot. Was that not sufficient evidence of the mores of a courtesan?

Madame Germont consoled herself with horseback rides and spending two months in Dieppe, which had just been adopted by the royal family.

Then Monsieur Germont died and left the enjoyment of Nointot and the usufruct of his entire fortune to his wife. The nephews nearly choked with rage, but the testament was in order, unassailable. It was therefore necessary for them to await the death of the slut, for she was much too clever to remarry. She had lost them an income of fifty thousand francs.

The town had not disarmed; on the contrary, it bristled with malevolence with regard to that fortune, which it considered as fraudulent. It made its cause that of the Germont heirs. In the province it is necessary not to touch property or family.

The widow made the decision of her isolation; she invited Rouenais for the hunting season. The château was full, for three months, of fanfares and the baying of hounds, and the rest of the time, to kill her ennui, she received the curé, the physician, and even the veterinarian and a few farmers at her table.

The region lent her lovers.

If opinion did not tuck up the soutane of the officiant of Nointot, it did not refrain from crumpling his ecclesiastical collar—Abbé Manjan was thirty-five years old and well made—and it was unscrupulous for her other acquaintances. She was stuck successively into the bed of the veterinarian Monsieur Tuboeuf, a muscular red-haired widower, freshly molded by the school of Alfortville, who cared for the livestock and the horses in the stable; the schoolteacher, Monsieur Daniel, although he was neither young nor tasty, with his squint and his sparse hair; and, simultaneously, all the farmers' sons. She was even credited with the stable-lads, and her coachman was not spared. Anyone in the château who had thick hair, shiny eyes and a hint of a moustache immediately obtained in public opinion Madame Germont's favors.

It is thus that a province takes its revenge, anonymously and in a cowardly fashion. Woe betide anyone who is unable to please it! They are pitilessly sacrificed.

Then fifty years had sounded for the widow. Still coquettish, Madame Germont had thrown herself into good works; devotion had been a port for her. With the first wrinkles and a little hair on the chin, it had been necessary to admit that it was finally God of whom Madame Germont went in search in church. Opinion softened slightly before her alms. The gift of a bell to the abbey of Monceux brought her closer to the town's drawing rooms. The senior clergy intervened. There was an exchange of visits between the château and a few houses at the New Year, Easter and carilloned feasts, but an avoidance of intimacy.

It was then that Aramin arrived, appropriately, to aliment the need for malevolent gossip and mockery by which the province was racked; it was a joy to complain about the old madwoman's latest caprice.

Madame Germont had brought back from Rouen a magnificent macaw, colored pale pink and bright blue, a veritable living flower, whose wings, tinted with pale yellow, were deployed like two flames, and all of whose colors seemed to flower in the sunlight and catch fire. The old lady had lavished on the parrot all the need for expansion of a tumultuous and justly suspected youth. She attached an extravagant affection to the creature.

As Monsieur Pintois, the justice of the peace, said, Caracalla was equaled. That woman was worthy of living under the Roman decadence; it was fetishism and worse: zoolatry, reeking of prostitution.

Aramin had an ebony perch and another in lemon-wood; he did not quit his mistress night or day. He slept in her dressing-room. A dismissed chambermaid swore that "in the bed, its black beak was beside Madame's head, on the same pillow." In any case, it ate at table with her, drinking from her glass and eating grapes from her lips. One might have thought that they were two lovers; the servants' parlor was scandalized. She sometimes took him with her to town in her coupé, and she had been seen descending at the suppliers' and sitting down in the shops with the parrot on her wrist: a spectacle without precedent, which caused children to form mobs outside the windows. She did not let a minute pass without kissing him.

His name was Aramin, like a Turk. A name of an emir for a parrot, that revealed well enough the soul of an odalisque! And, a final folly, in order to take him for walks, she had a golden chain made, decorated with rubies, which a jade ring fixed to his foot.

It was the precious Aramin who had disappeared, on the fourteenth of July, during the firework display on the château lawn. An unfortunate rocket, fallen in the dressing room through an open window, had set fire to Madame Germont's peignoirs, and the whole wardrobe had gone up in flames. Aramin must have been roasted too, for he was never seen again.

It was thought for a long time that he had fled through the window and gained the shelter of the park. The inconsolable Madame Germont had nursed that hope for a while. The entire domain was searched, then the countryside—the woods and the farms—was beaten. The search had been extended as far as the neighboring communes. Aramin was advertised by the gamekeepers, in the village squares, and large rewards were loudly clarioned. A new phoenix, Aramin had never reappeared.

Aldric Gromare, at table in the Branche de Houx between the blacksmith Malroux and the wigmaker Bricou, concluded his investigation. His brain some-what upset by emotion, and also by a few glasses of liqueur, Aldric now understood what voice it was that had opined that rain would fall that evening, that the meadows were green and that the sky was dark, when Babaud Monier and the other old women were deceived while looking at the cat Mirou, sorcerer and ventriloquist. He also knew why the frightful bird of ill-omen that had made a racket in the grain-loft, and had been nailed to the batten of the door like a caster of malevolent spells, and had his feathers reddened and blackened by flames. The beast had escaped from a conflagration, not from Hell. Poor Aramin, surprised and blinded by the fire, had flown in panic into the countryside; he had fled under the nocturnal sky, be-wildered and terrified, always straight ahead, and at dawn had taken refuge through an open skylight in Babaud Monier's grain-loft.

Brutalized by terror, he had remained there for a month, hiding in the shadows, nourishing himself on the grain and fruits stored there. At times he had jabbered phrases learned parrot-fashion, until the day when the popular creature had been charged with the crimes lent to Mirou, the sorcerer cat.

"Poor beast! Oh, surely I won't tell Madame anything; she loved him like her child. She'd be capable of perishing if she knew what her Aramin had endured. They made him suffer here, they made him suffer! Oh, the brutes!"

And he withdrew, after having paid for the rounds.

Aldric Gromare resumed the route to the farm, but like a wily man, as soon as night fell, he retraced his steps, went into the Clos Muré, detached the pitiful skeleton and carried it away, preciously nested in his blouse.

A short time later, he found it, as if by accident, in the framework of one of his barns, and with a thousand precautions, he informed the good Madame Germont. The latter dissolved in tears, demanded to see the dear remains, suffered a crisis of nerves before the horrible thing, and decided to have it incinerated.

An alabaster urn received the ashes of the martyred bird. It still ornaments the mantelpiece of Madame Germont's bedroom.

For having found the remains of Aramin in his barn, Master Aldric Gromare had his annual rent reduced by five francs.

Moral: it is always necessary to deceive generous hearts. There is no happiness without lies.

HOGUEMORE

THE fantastic aspect of animals, their mysterious and sometimes efficacious role in the grave or definitive circumstances of our lives, their quasi-tutelary intervention at the dangerous turnings of certain existences; their seemingly providential appearances; of all these strange, unexpected and inexplicable things in which the naivety of childlike peoples would like to see the presence of fays and gods, I felt the effects profoundly one day, and in an intoxicated stupor of fear I have been able to measure, by the power of the sudden enchantment, how vivacious the Aryan race still is in a Norman schoolboy.

I might have been twelve or thirteen years old. I was interned in a lycée in Paris, the Henri IV, I believe: the Lycée Henri IV, the playgrounds of which felt the thin or dense shadow of the old Clovis tower floating over them. I spent the long vacations in Normandy, a month with my parents in the little coastal town where I grew up; a fortnight with my grandmother in the environs of Rouen; and the last fortnight in September with one of my father's sisters, a widow with a daughter five years younger than me, my aunt Epresménil.

My aunt Epresménil, blonde, pale and interesting, with her English curls and her eternal black crepe, lived on the high plateaux of Criqueboeuf, between Étretat and Le Havre, in a kind of château surrounded by farms—which did not prevent my aunt's domain from being the saddest and most isolated in the region.

The château was named Hoguemore, and the property had all the melancholy of that name. Was it the neighborhood of the sea, the great breath of which could be felt unfurling, and which put a taste of salt into the leaves, or the infinite distress of all those plowed fields, in the midst of which Hoguemore seemed an island, circled for two leagues around by cultures of flax, rye, lucerne and rapeseed? In the middle of that ocean of crops, however, before the bleak extent of those plains, limited to the west by the Manche, from which jutted rare village steeples at the four cardinal points, my cousin Cécile and I perished of ennui in Hoguemore; the windswept location of which, it was claimed, had a perfect salubrity for our young lungs.

To tell the truth, Hoguemore was more of a country house than a château. Although built in 1840, the dwelling was in the Louis XIII style. Fine stonework stood out from the pink of bricks and a double projection swelled each extremity of the house, taking the place of towers. An immense perron of five steps raised Hoguemore throughout its length; all the rooms of the ground floor opened on to the perron by way of high door-windows and strong interior shutters did not pre-

148

vent the low-ceilinged drawing rooms from giving the impression of being inside a lantern, with views of the park framed in all the windows.

All that made Hoguemore a rather lugubrious place, but its distress, for me, was above all in its horizons; those immutable horizons of plowed fields, which appeared at the end of a pathway, or the extremity of a lawn, making the park an islet of verdure in the heart of the monotony of the fields.

All those sadnesses suited the beauty of my aunt d'Epresménil; her languor of a dreamy and indolent blonde, heightened by her veils of mourning, found an appropriate frame in the haughty rooms of Hoguemore. My aunt d'Epresménil was no more than twenty-eight years old, my cousin Cécile was six. Romantic, with the sentimental and slightly silly romanticism of the epoch, and a great reader of George Sand, my aunt d'Epresménil devoured all the novels of Feuillet[1] and stayed up late into the night playing Chopin and Schumann on the piano. She paraded her regrets gracefully, perhaps more for the gallery than love of her late husband, who had made her very unhappy, and with no affectation, but because, being very feminine, she made an attitude out of her grief.

In the locale people called her "the Widow." A profound respect surrounded Madame d'Epresménil.

That widowhood, nobly borne, might have led her, a few years earlier, to a rich marriage. My aunt

---

1 Like the author, the relentlessly neurotic Octave Feuillet (1821-1890) was born in Normandy.

Epresménil could have picked up three millions in the train of her mourning-dress; the suitors of the province appreciate faithful women.

For the moment my aunt d'Epresménil, somewhat captive of her farmers, who would have paid her rather poorly if they had not sensed her on their back, spent eight months of the year at Hoguemore. My uncle d'Epresménil had encumbered his wealth somewhat with mortgages, and the young woman had the courage to extinguish them. She was a headstrong woman, who, sentimental as she was, knew that there is nothing without an established situation, and Normandy, above all, loves reliable placements and clear incomes.

She was sacrificing herself, she said, to her daughter, and for that reason lived at Hoguemore, where she scarcely amused herself. I even think, between ourselves, that she was dying of fear there.

The dwelling was one of the most isolated; five hundred meters separated it from the nearest farmhouse, and the personnel of the château was minimal, again for reasons of economy. The men slept in the outbuildings, above the stables, with the exception of Jean, the valet de chambre, who was lodged under the eaves with the chambermaid and the cook. There was, therefore, only one man in the château, for my twelve years hardly counted, and I only spent two weeks a year at Hoguemore.

The house was thus occupied by four women, confided to the guard of Jean.

My aunt found that guard insufficient herself, for, when night fell, we scarcely lingered in the drawing rooms of the ground floor. Once the dessert had been expedited, while the table was not yet cleared, we went upstairs to my aunt's bedroom, which, vast and airy, with exactly the same proportions as the drawing room, commanded the whole of the first floor landing and opened the two battens of its door over the steps of the main staircase.

On emerging from her room in the morning, Madame d'Epresménil embraced with her gaze the enormous stairwell, all the way to the panoplies of the vestibule below, reflected in the back and white checkerboard of the floor tiles.

I occupied a small room beside my aunt's; we went upstairs at half past eight. Cécile was put to bed at nine. Madame d'Epresménil tolerated me until ten, and while, plunged in some illustrated book, I was impassioned by the unmerited woes of a suspected courage or a misconceived virtue, my aunt, seated at the piano, deceived the aspirations of her romantic and deprived soul with some waltz by Chopin or some reverie by Schumann.

One evening—it was the twenty-fifth of September—the weather had been heavy with an impending storm all day. In the park, numbed by heat, where not a breath of wind stirred a leaf, we had remained until four o'clock, my aunt, my cousin and I, taking refuge in the darkest part of the wood; the green shade gave more freshness there. It was impossible to stay in the château; one breathed fire in the drawing rooms, fire on the lawns and in the uncovered pathways; and in the dry and burning weather one had a thirst that nothing could extinguish, an oppressive anguish, under a low yellow sky—a sky one might have thought obscured by ash, the false lightning of which recalled that of the Primitives in the agonies of Golgotha.

At about five o'clock, large raindrops began to fall, and then a torrential rain. We were obliged to go back to the house under a stinging downpour; the sky had split, with rumbles and crashes of thunder and flashes of lightning. Now, in the park, haunted by an odor of ozone, there was the din of raindrops dripping from leaf to leaf, the damp and seemingly appeased breath of the glad foliage, a joy of rejuvenation of the moist country-side, and in the washed sky, swept by clouds the color of nacre, the limpidity of a crystalline moonlight.

Oh, that September moonlight after that stormy evening! How far one could see, over the plateau of the farms!

My aunt and I were in her bedroom. Through the wide-open windows a fine odor rose of wet ivy and honeysuckle. It must have been very late, a little after eleven o'clock. In the sleeping house, my aunt d'Epresménil allowed me to read in company with her. She had not touched the piano that evening; the rain had relaxed her benevolently, and like a large bloom-ing flower, silent and soft, she abandoned herself to the silence and the night.

I was reading. It was, I remember, a story of fays, the hallucinating and impassioning story of a princess wandering and fugitive through the perilous regions of an enemy realm; Florimonde had fled, carried away involuntarily in the wind of a panic, her routed armies

152

had dragged her and her war chariot into unknown territory. Assailed there by savage hordes, she had only owed her salvation to the devotion of her nurse, and had fled across country. She had scaled hedges and crossed ditches for days and nights, prowling through marshes and along bogs haunted by strange fire follets. Now she had reached a wood, a damp and ruddy November wood, with old trees clad in moss, where the soil sweated and screeched underfoot. In that rotten and greasy wood, she followed an avenue of tall trees between high banks, an obscure and straight avenue that plunged into a darkness denser from hour to hour, interminably, and from hour to hour the damp soil stuck to her footfalls more.

Mysterious pathway! The sticky soil was now shifting in a disquieting fashion. A filthy swarm was pullulating beneath her feet; little black forms, leaping over the path with a single bound, were crossing from one bank to the other. Viscous and cold, the princess felt them climbing up her ankles and falling back into the grass with a soft sound. Amid all those vaguely animate and flaccid things, that crawling and semi-jumping, the nauseated princess felt herself weakening. The obscure path was invaded by toads; they were legion; they populated the hollows of roots and the soft grassy banks. She now had them up to her knees, and in the autumnal darkness there was a moving and innumerable tide.

Then, in the silence of the deserted house a plaintive and soft cry was suddenly audible, and at the same time, we heard the friction of something heavy and soft coming up the stairs.

My temples were moist; my aunt had straightened up, very pale. Deliberately, she opened the door that overlooked the main stairway. The steps were all white with moonlight. Down below, in the vestibule, the entrance door was wide open to the enchantment of the park. On the steps of the staircase, something gray was ascending heavily.

A toad was there, its little paws climbing each step with difficulty; its pale belly was displayed, flaccid, as it posed there. The beast had evidently come from outside. But who had opened the door on the ground floor? My aunt looked at the clock; it marked ten to midnight. There was someone in the house; a malefactor, perhaps several, had introduced himself into the dwelling and we were alone with two women and old Jean.

My aunt rang, and rang again. Exasperated carillons filled the whole house. The maids took a long time to come down. Down below, running footsteps could be heard in the drawing rooms. We dared not make a move. The cook came down first. The sight of the open door froze her; then came Rosa, the chambermaid. Jean should have got out of bed, for the ringing was loud, but he did not come. My aunt, having seized an old pistol, strove to maneuver the firing mechanism. On the landing the domestics were fainting, half-dead. And the toad was still climbing up. The dwelling appeared magnified by the silence. Teeth could be heard clicking in terror.

Down below, the coming and goings ceased. Suddenly, a noise of broken windows faded away in a racket of closing shutters.

It was a terrible night. The next day, we found the servants' parlor and the dining room ransacked; all the silverware had been stolen and a Boulle clock to which my aunt attached a great value. The malefactors, disturbed by my aunt's exasperated ringing, had fled through a window in the servants' parlor. Jean, the old valet, was found drowned in a ditch in the park. He ran after women; he must have been drawn outside by the appeal of some skirt. His habits were known; the malefactors were local.

What would have become of us if the providential toad had not raised the alarm?

The coincidence of that hallucinatory reading and that tutelary intervention of a toad? There are, in certain hazards, undeniable affinities.

THE GEESE OF PIROU

L AST autumn I spent a fortnight staying with a friend in Low Normandy, between Coutances and Lessay.

Today, Bélin lives retired in Cotentin. The country is picturesque and sad, eternally beaten by the westerly wind, which makes the sea restless and sweeps the sky with big gray clouds: the skies of anger and distress, the vision of which the painter Collet fixed so imperiously in his Breton studies. Between an ocean the color of bile—so many reefs are tangled with wrack there, in troubled and sandy water—and the monotony of desperately green pasturelands, we spent the time making excursions in the surrounding area. It is necessary to kill the hours during those long rural autumn days! There was not a week when my friend Maurice Bélin did not take me at least three times to visit some ruined abbey or château: Medieval vestiges of historical splendors, the number of which still attests to the interminable struggles of the autochthons against the Norman invaders.

Thus, we had visited the Château d'Argouges, where a popular legend places the heroic legend of the Fay. The legend is almost the same as that of the legend of Mélusine in Lusignan.

Like Lusignan, a sire d'Argouges, returning from hunting one evening, encounters on the bank of a spring a lady of marvelous beauty. He falls in love with her and marries her, under the express condition that he never pronounces the word "Death." The amorous d'Argouges keeps his promise and the mysterious spouse gives him several children, until the morning when, chagrined by waiting for an hour for his wife to complete her adornment, he says to the Comtesse: "Beautiful lady, be good enough to seek Death, for you're taking a long time in your task." With a heart-rending cry, as if he had dealt her a mortal blow, the fay of Argouges evaporates in the air. As she flees she leaves the imprint of her hand on the door of the château. The lamentable cries of the victim still resound in the ruins of Argouges. "Death! Death!" weeps the fay's agonized soul by night, under the winter stars and the April moon.

It is very similar, I repeat, to the legend of Lusignan; it is also, dramatized by the Middle Ages, the exquisite fable of Psyche: the transgressed order leads to the destruction of the cherished being.

After Argouges we visited Bânes, where popular dreaming has embroidered almost the same legend, this time lending it to Marguerite de Champagne, the wife of Philippe d'Argouges, Seigneur de Crutot, and it thus that the same imaginations are reincarnated through time and space, in accordance with the terrain or the race, in different figures. They are only apparently different, for the human soul is identical—and in all climates, Nordic mythology, Greek mythology or Hindu pantheism, humans have almost a unique conception of beauty and symbolism.

My friend Maurice Bélin is a normanizing Norman, besotted with his Normandy and fanatical about its traditions. He did not spare me any, and, being very erudite, he annotated, so to speak, every landscape with some fabulous or melancholy tale. Nostalgia had ended up gripping my heart. The sadness of the high plateaux and the solitude of their fields of gorse and furze reddened by the westerly wind, the isolation of the little abandoned creeks, espoused until the level of the rock by a sly and savage sea, the eternal mourning of those turbulent and low skies, and even the dolorous stupor of the old convulsed and twisted apple trees: all of that chastised nature in revolt against the rudeness of a hostile climate had ended up by darkening my ideas and weaving within me a funereal fabric of dreams and regrets, a marvelous canvas for the magical blossoming of phantoms of the past.

It is on that incomparable state of mind, born of the ambience of beings and things, that the tellers of legends, who are embroiderers in their fashion, establish the most beautiful tapestries of the romantic and the marvelous.

One evening, when we were returning to Lessay in one of those equivocal—I might even say sorcerous—dusks, which lend a strange character to the entire landscape, making tree-trunks threaten and rocks snigger, one of those wicked dusks that deform, alter and transform, and make you desire, on the horizon, silhouettes of keeps and crenellated bell-towers, we emerged from a bend in the road in front of a small hill—less than a hill, a mound—crimson-tinted by heather, on which, among the vague earthen debris, fragments of wall and a collapsed tower were divinable.

The sky was as red as a wound, with streaks of greenish gold of the most sulfurous aspect. On that sinister horizon the ruin was imposing, glowering and grandiose, lying in ambush there in that solitude, like a spell-casting fay. Even our mounts—we were on horseback—pricked up their ears and stopped. Then Maurice designated the old walls to me.

"Pirou![1] One of the oldest châteaux in the region, and also one of the strangest legends. It was inhabited by fays. Those fays were the daughters of a great seigneur of the time; they had built the Château de Pirou many years before the Norman invasion, and they spent their days there in the most edifying community, cultivating simples, composing philters, crushing unguents and making magical conjurations in order to aid the poor, the sick and traveling pilgrims in distress. They were already old when the first pirate ships appeared off the coast. Troubled in their solitude by the descent of the Normans and fearful of the violence of the barbarians,

---

1 Since this story was written the Château de Pirou has been considerably restored and is nowadays a tourist attraction; the legend retold here, which was obscure when the story was penned, has also been "restored" along with the edifice.

they imagined, in order to protect themselves from it transforming themselves into wild geese.

"At the sight of the first pointed helmet of the invaders, the fays of Pirou took flight as wild geese! There is nothing like old age and experience for inventing such admirable precautions! In spite of their metamorphosis, the fays of Pirou did not abandon their dwelling. During the centuries, on the first of March every year, a flock of wild geese returned to inhabit the nests that they had hollowed out in the walls of the château.

"There is more. Vigneul-Marville,[1] from whom I am borrowing these details, adds this: 'When a son is born in the illustrious house of Pirou, the males of these geese, displaying their moist beautiful gray plumes take the height of the pavement in the courtyards of the château; but when a daughter is born, the females, in plumage whiter than snow, take priority over the males. If the daughter is to become a nun, one of those geese is remarked among the others, which does not build a nest but remains solitary in a corner, eating little and sighing in her heart.'

"But that legend is similar to many others. More than twenty years ago, village boors destroyed the wall of the nests of the seigneurial geese; the ruins only shelter ospreys now. The gods go away and human pride is consoled in consequence, but the tender and the

1 "Vigneul-Marville" was one of the pseudonyms of a French monk of the seventeenth century, originally known as Noël Argonne, who initially took the name of Bonaventure in religion. His *Mélanges d'histoire et de littérature* was published the three volumes in 1699-1701.

imaginative sense the emptiness of the hours weighing more dolorously in a time that is henceforth devoid of symbols and faith.

"Chimerical, if you wish, that I grant you, but so sympathetic to the sadness of our destinies, the fays should never have gone away without return. It was a relief to believe in them. The lie is the sole reason for living; there are so many dolors down here to lament and to lighten!"

Our horses had picked up their pace again, and the first roofs of Lessay stood out in denser shadows against the gray of the night.

It was a melancholy return.

Hazard determined that at dinner, Maurice's cook served us a goose. Dressed with onions, chestnuts and thyme, it was golden and juicy.

"The last fay of Pirou!" I said, making allusion to our excursion.

"Don't mock," said my host, "you'll make trouble for me with my cook. Anastasie is quite capable of quitting me. The geese of Pirou are very popular and the low people still believe in them. Oh, superstition is tenacious. It's only ten years since their memory claimed another victim in Barqueville, a little hamlet near Lessay. We traversed it in order to reenter the town.

"No! What are you telling me?"

"The exact truth. The geese of Pirou caused a poor poultry merchant to lose her head and sent her to the hospice in Lessay. I believe that Mère Bailhache is still there."

"Mère Bailhache has seen the fays?"

"Mère Bailhache has seen more than the fays; she has seen her own geese . . . but in such conditions that you and I would have howled in fear. It's an utterly Hoffmannesque story. A wholly unexpected combination of circumstances contrived a reality more frightening than a fantastic tale. Anyone here can tell it to you. Anyway, this is it:

"Mère Bailhache, a farmer's wife, was notorious in the markets of Lessay and Coutances. For forty years she brought her poultry on Saturday and Wednesday. I've always known her; since my earliest childhood I stopped before her large baskets full of the cheeping of chickens and the quacking of ducks. Mère Bailhache was almost a power; she had the finest clientele in Lessay, and if she didn't remember a cook's face she often refused to sell to them. She was wheezy and eccentric; she didn't tolerate haggling, and treated the richest ladies in the parish as equals; but with her one was always certain of being well served. She had a fashion of making you feel the rump of a fowl that brooked no reply. Madame Bailhache was the official supplier of the upper class. People made use of her from father to son; she did not want to sell to hotels. My grandmother and my mother always bought the Christmas goose and the Easter turkey from her.

"Popular as the geese of Pirou are here, people are no less fond of the flesh of their peers; goose is, in this region, the classic dish and the fare of carilloned winter feasts: Christmas geese, New Year geese and Epiphany geese. Mère Bailhache always furnished the finest, and they were not only those from her farm that she paraded in the markets, but also those of the surrounding area, which she carried off two months in advance in order to fatten them up.

"In the winter of '92, which was, as you know, very rigorous. Mère Bailhache found herself at the head of a flock of geese and ganders such as she had not had for several years. Christmas fell on a Friday. The Lessay market held on Wednesday was for her a day of great sales. She took ten geese from her flock, the fattest and readiest, and in order not to have to pursue them and seize them on the morning of the market, in order to bring them to the clients very white and clean, she had the idea of shutting them in her pantry. 'Go on, then, splash in your puddles now, dirty beasts!'

"And, delighted with her invention, with a turn of the key in the lock, she got on with the farm chores. That happened on Monday evening, two days before market day.

"On the Tuesday, about four o'clock, Mère Bailhache had the curiosity to go and see how her beasts were getting on. She picked up her bunch of keys again, put one in the lock and opened the door. What a spectacle! The ten geese were lying inanimate, necks limp, eyes extinct, wings half open, some on their belly and others on their back. Mère Bailhache's ten geese, the fine flower of her poultry-yard, were lying on the beaten earth of the pantry. 'Jesus Maria!' cried the old woman. 'A spell has been cast on them! Or is it a weasel that has killed them?'

"She put her hands together, lifted her arms to the heavens and roused the farmhands and maidservants.

"There was no trace of blood, so it wasn't weasels. All the geese were still warm; their feet had not yet stiffened. They had eaten too much, for their bellies were round—those animals are so voracious.

"And as Mère Bailhache, a shrewd Norman, didn't want to lose the benefit of her geese, she immediately set about plucking them, installing all the servants in the task. The beasts still being warm, it was necessary to take advantage of it. She would take them to Lessay all naked and adorned, as merchants of comestibles sell them; she could permit herself that; her clients would see no malice in it, and it would delight the cooks.

So, the geese are plucked, but as nothing freezes more easily than dead birds, it was the twenty-first of December, and the dead fowl might attract rats, Mère Bailhahe had the idea of having the ten geese taken to her bedroom; she would keep an eye on them while sleeping, it was already quite enough that they were dead.

"The geese were heaped up in a corner. Mère Bailhache signed herself, got into bed, blew out the candle and went to sleep.

The bedroom window was unshuttered and devoid of curtains; winter moonlight was illuminating the whole room.

Toward midnight, a faint rustling, a sound of soft footfalls, whimpers and then plaints wake the old woman with a start. A swarm of white forms fills one corner of her bedroom; they are nameless nudities, such as one sees in nightmares: granular thighs, wings and bellies. They are crawling, trying to fly and hopping in an obscene entanglement, with plaintive cries and bizarre torsions; they are the winged toads of the *Tentations de Saint Antoine* and the gnomes with birds' necks of Goya's *Sabbats*.

Mère Bailhache, her eyes wide with terror, thinks that the Devil is in her bedroom. Long plumed necks extend toward her bed, beaks menace her and others bite her sheets, and in that horde of hopping, contorted and pale beasts, Mère Bailhache recognizes the specters of her geese, her plucked and resuscitated beasts, phantasmal, alarming, almost apocalyptically unexpected and terrible.

"'The geese of Pirou!'

"The farmhands who come running in response to her cries find her clicking her teeth and repeating that unique phrase with the tenacity of a lunatic: 'The geese of Pirou!'

"Mère Bailhache never recovered her reason; she had to be put in the hospice. The geese of Pirou are still tormenting her there

"What about the geese, you say, those unfortunate magical geese—what had plunged them into that strange death-like sleep? They had done it themselves. While going crazy in the cellar, where Mère Bailhache had put her winter provisions, they had knocked over a large bottle of cherries in brandy; the bottle had broken, the cherries had scattered, and, gluttonous as they are, the geese had thrown themselves on the windfall and had got drunk like natural individuals. It was dead drunk that they had been found by the farmer, and in her stupor, without even looking to see where the debris

166

came from, it was dead drunk that Mère Bailhache had had them plucked and transported to her bedroom.

"Gradually sobered up, and reanimated by the sensation of pain, the unfortunate geese, plucked alive, had woken the poor woman up in the middle of the night with their movements and their cries."

The geese of Pirou! It requires no more to accredit a legend.

A GAME OF SHUTTLECOCK

WE were at Saint-Agricol.

As we quit the last step of its curious perron, a carriage stopped there, a master carriage such as one only sees in the provinces, obsolete in form, simultaneously too large and too low, and rather poorly suspended on its springs: one of those antique berlines that, relegated to old garages, see chickens perching on their banquettes and sometimes play host to broods of ducks; I will spare you the cobwebs.

This one had the advantage of being relatively well-kept. Its coachman, engulfed in a long overcoat, had no moustache; he had the impersonal and glabrous face of the domestics of a good house. The brasses of the harness glistened; the two horses had shiny coats. For the province and the Midi, the negligence of which is legendary, it was a rig of the utmost luxury.

A little groom tumbled from the seat and opened the door respectfully. An old lady of importance and weight got down. All the authority of deep wealth was displayed in the sunlight for a long time and all the

169

majesty of a hereditary fortune were affirmed in the lady's gait and attire.

Not ugly, besides: the plump and reposed figure of an abbess of the previous century, a pretty profile thickened by forty years, and admirable eyes, Provençal eyes with velvety dark irises, the brightness of which was deadened by a studied gaze.

"Severin, you'll take Mademoiselle to the convent and came back here in half an hour."

The groom had closed the door again, and with a stride that was still supple, in spite of her stoutness, the lady climbed the perron of the church. She passed close to us without seeing us. Her long lowered eyelids had not deigned to lift the curtain of their lashes for us; she plunged under the porch.

"Eh!" said my friend Marius Laparède. "Did you see her? Oh, the king isn't her cousin! What a figurehead for a ship's prow, eh? She creaks more on making landfall than the timbers of a ship that has seen all ports!"

"Rich?"

"Need you ask? She reeks of millions. That arrogance. She's prouder than a censer. That's Madame Cambares, the lady of Les Platanes, the most beautiful domain in Avignon; I'll take you there. Oh, the view one has from there over the valley of the Rhône is almost as beautiful as the panorama of the Dom. You can't see Villeneuve, that's the only difference; but you discover Sorgues and Barbentane, and what an avenue of trees, my friend! One is cool there in the full midday. The wind of the Ventoux sweeps the terrace. In mid-August you think you're respiring the sea breeze, the lungs dilate as they do on the jetty at Marseille. It's that pretentious woman, that mutterer of prayers and bad arguments—you've seen how she talks to her servants—who possesses the Cambares house today, and the avenue of plane trees, and the olive grove, and the flower garden, and the pond with all its fish. Oh, as beautiful domains go, it's a beautiful domain. If you'd had seen the collection of poppies that the father-in-law, Honorat Cambares, cultivated there! Double poppies the size of cabbage-flowers. They were brought from Tarascon and Beacaire, even Arles—what am I saying?—from Aix and Salon, in the times when they were in flower. And that prude makes the law for the town! The whole country is at her feet. If that isn't a shame! A granddaughter of Trestaillon!"

"Who's Trestaillon?"

"The assassin of Maréchal Brune,[1] the man who led the rabble to the Hôtel du Palais-Royal, where he was killed, poor fellow. He was taken out of his berline at the Porte de l'Oulle; I showed you the house on the little square; there's a fountain in the courtyard. Trestaillon was a worker—a tanner or a butcher, I'm

---

1 Guillaume Brune (1763-1815) was a prominent Revolutionary and soldier, murdered in Avignon during the so-called White Terror in the early days of the Bourbon Restoration. History does not, in fact, record confidently that he was murdered by the notorious Jacques Dupont, nicknamed "Trestaillons," although the latter certainly led murderous gangs during the White Terror, and he was credited with a key role in the assassination in the melodrama *Le Maréchal Brune, ou le terreur de 1815* (1831) by Charles Desire and Fontan Depeuty, which Lorrain might well have read or seen performed.

not sure which. At any rate he handled beasts, stunned them alive or, dead, ground their skins. Well, Madame Cambares, the one you saw, Trestaillon's daughter was her grandmother."

"No!"

"As I tell you."

"But then, the marriage . . . "

"Oh, that's a whole story. The marriage was a stroke of luck, an unexpected hazard that Clara Balure had. Yes, Clara Balure was Madame Cambares' name as a young woman. She married the son and Les Platanes and the million, and all that thanks to a game of shuttlecock. Oh, it was a fine stroke of the racquet that the little Trestaillon gave that morning!"

"If you'd care to explain, Marius, beginning at the beginning: you're confusing me, and I don't understand any of it."

"Well, this is it!"

And my friend Marius took me by the arm.

"Clara Balure, the woman we've just seen, was the daughter of a keeper of mortgages. Her worthy father, who only had his job, and wasn't from the region, had married a Mademoiselle Stéphanie Malitourne here, the daughter of a Malitourne who had a café on the Place Pétrarque, and without malice, the poor fellow, because that Malitourne had married Trestaillon's daughter, and although his affairs prospered, he wasn't esteemed in the locale.

"The son-in-law of an assassin is immediately known in all small towns. I know that Trestaillon wasn't the only one to carry out the coup, but he's the only one named in the histories. There were surely other guilty men, but all the unknown Trestaillons were only too glad to have the historic Trestaillon in order to rehabilitate themselves on his back."

"For the cowardice of peoples is their justice! You're eminently philosophical, Marius."

"So, Père Balure, in his quality as a newcomer in the region, let himself be led up the garden path by Père Malitourne and his daughter, who was a fine sprig of a woman, in the genre of Madame Cambares. He married, then, and founded a family in little Clara Balure. As he was a perfectly honest man, obliging to everyone and couldn't have been milder in his relationship, and cultivated with it, passionate about Roman antiquities; and as Madame Balure, née Malitourne had a perfect appearance, and sufficient devotion that nothing was ever whispered about her and she had brought her daughter up strictly, people were quite willing to forget the Trestaillon somewhat, and society, departing from its rigor, consented to receive them. It's also necessary to say that little Clara Balure was adorably pretty, as white as milk, with dark caressing eyes, large eyes with lustrous lashes like a bird's plumage, and a fresh mouth . . . a cherry that opened over the enamel of little teeth! She was a true daughter of Provence, one of Mistral's *Mireïos*,[1] next to whom every man senses himself a male, one of those creatures simultaneously Greek and Saracen scented by the idyll, amour and the

---

1 Frédéric Mistral's epic poem *Mirèio* (1859) became the basis of Charles Gounod's opera *Mireille* (1864).

sun. She had a true grace, little Balure, and the father and mother were invited everywhere in order to have their daughter.

"Les Platanes was one of the houses where the keeper of mortgages was fêted the most. Madame Honorat Cambares, left a widow with a son and two daughters, had been seized by a fine owner's passion for Achille Balure, who, on the strength of his archeological knowledge, had discovered vestiges of a Roman villa in Les Platanes. With that, the meridional imagination of Madame Cambares had caught fire. The worthy lady no longer dreamed about anything but tricliniums, impluviums, tripods, bas-reliefs, old bronzes and frescos that all the museums of France and Europe would dispute at a price of gold. She imagined treading underfoot a new Pompeii; the terraces of Les Platanes, concealed treasures. She consulted and annotated volumes in the company of Monsieur Balure, but didn't decide on excavations; it would have overturned three terraces, and the minority of her daughters retained her, but the intimacy of the Cambares and the Balures was considerable. Similar hopes were entertained for them, fortune for the former, glory for the latter. The keeper of mortgages and his family dined at Les Platanes at least twice a week.

"The house was, in any case, largely open. It was a family tradition of the Cambares to receive all of Avignon society on Sunday. People came after vespers to respire the good air of the terraces. The men strolled under the plane trees, the women chatted in the drawing room, the young women played in the garden; at five o'clock, Madame Cambares offered a collation; raisin toast and butter in winter and, in their season, cherries or peaches, the produce of the kitchen garden.

"It was an honor to be received at Les Platanes. In Avignon. Madame Cambares' Sundays had class. In view of the age of her daughters, Madame Cambares had extended her invitations. Lydie and Thérèse were not yet ready to marry; Lydie was twenty and Thérèse eighteen. Their mother was not in difficulty, they were each worth half a million francs of dowry; but Madame Cambares made sure that her daughters had an escort of companions; the demoiselles Cambares set the tone for society.

"Their simplicity was proverbial. Madame Cambares claimed that it was only people without a sou who tried to impose by means of external elegance. Organdie and jaconas triumphed at Les Platanes. The same dresses were seen there for three years; in any case, why put expense into coquetry? As a prudent mother, Madame Cambares did not invite any young men; the brothers of the young women of the circle were only admitted under sixteen years of age. Madame Cambares was counting on not marrying Lydie and Thérèse in Avignon.

"Nor was the brother of the demoiselles seen: Olivier Cambares, a kind of red-headed giant with thick curly hair à la Lucius Verus;[1] entirely a portrait of his grandfather Aristide Roumestan. Olivier Cambares

---

1 Lucius Verus was the co-emperor of Rome with his more famous adoptive brother Marcus Aurelius. His bust credited him with a remarkable fleece of curly hair.

was a veritable bear, uniquely preoccupied with hunting and fishing, and whom even the grisettes of the old town had not succeeded in winkling out, in spite of his twenty-five years. He only took pleasure with common folk and spent the best part of his time with the boatmen of the Rhône. He went up or down the river with them and stayed for three or four days without returning to Les Platanes, where his mother did not worry about those absences. It was said that the Cambares son was a little simple, and Madame Cambares did not care overmuch to exhibit him to her acquaintances. Olivier shone by his absence at all his mother's gatherings. On the other hand, his strength was legendary among all the river-dwellers. Olivier delighted all the humble people with his prowess: a great drinker and a great eater, he had all the qualities that please the rabble, save that he was cold with women, and that was one of the amazements of the region, still simple-minded.

"Those Sundays at Les Platanes! Clara Balure was the joy and the ball-roller. Lively, mischievous, with large eyes of imperturbable innocence . . . the misfortune was that there was nothing natural about her. A simpering coquette, she always contrived, during games of shuttlecock and graces, to throw her hoop or drop her racquet in the direction of the messieurs, where her irruption always gave rise to flattering murmurs.

"It was during one of those games that the misadventure happened to her that made Clara Balure into Madame Cambares. The demoiselles were playing on the ultimate terrace, adjacent to the vegetable garden. Clara's shuttlecock, launched at top speed by a brisk

176

thrust of the racquet, went to fall on the side of the commons, in the middle of a fenced-off sewage tank. Clara launched herself recklessly in quest of her shuttlecock; she was lured by the solidity of what she mistook for soil; Lydie and Thérèse tried in vain to retain her.

"The headstrong Clara has faith in her lightness, and with the grace of a dancer she risks herself inside the enclosure; the sewage gives way under her weight. Clara Balure sinks up to her knees in a sticky substance, the stench of which informs her too late of where she is. There is a rapid immersion in a pool of filthy fluid; Clara Balure is soon up to her neck. She clings desperately to the frail palisade; Les Platanes resounds with her screams; the demoiselles shout for help, the relatives come running and the staff too. The unfortunate Clara is pulled out of that rustic sewer in time, but my God, in what a state! 'Poor child! A little more and she would have asphyxiated!'

"Quickly, Madame Cambares gives orders. A bath is warmed up and the pitiful Clara is transported to the laundry, semi-conscious, fetid and wrapped in blankets. She is plunged into the bath and the water is renewed three times; she is soaped, she is scrubbed, she is perfumed, and when she has recovered somewhat from her fright she is left alone with warm linen.

"Clara was emerging like a young nymph from the reparative bath when, by the purest of coincidences, Olivier Cambares came into the laundry. He had been absent since dawn and knew nothing about the event. He was coming to put away his fishing equipment.

"Clara sees that red beard and green eyes, and utters a scream, folding her arms over her young bosom. Olivier's eyes open wide; he blushes, stammers, and only just has time to take a step forward to receive the fainting young woman in his arms. It was too much emotion for one day. But the clan of mothers is on watch outside the laundry. Madame Cambares rushes in, and Madame Balure too. They find Clara inanimate and naked on Olivier's heaving torso.

"It was necessary to marry those children!

"In any case, Olivier declared that same evening that he would only marry Monsieur Balure's daughter. And that is why the granddaughter of Trestaillon is today the lady of Les Platanes. As with many others, m*** brought her luck."[1]

---

1 As previously noted, *merdre* is a stronger expletive in French than *shit* is in English.

A COUNTRY EXCURSION

"IT is necessary not to believe that successful marriages are habitual hereabouts. It is not sufficient for daughters in quest of marriage-partners to show a corner of their skin, or even all of it, to fish up a million and a husband's name. Monsieur Cambares, whom little Clara Balure lifted so nimbly by stepping out of her bath and shoving her two young breasts in his face in a faint, unconscious or otherwise, was nothing less than resourceful. The quivering nudity of the pretty bather was a thunderbolt for him because it was a revelation. A more enlightened fellow would probably have picked the flower without going to the altar in order to do so.

"Trestaillon's granddaughter was lucky; not all the local girls have that good fortune, and I know one whose skirt being lifted above the knee—and that involuntarily, poor thing—cost her a fine marriage. What she showed that day of her youth—the child was seventeen years old—alarmed the fiancé so much that the engagement was broken off. The girl was, however, charming and any other would have been enticed, if not dazzled—but the fellow was a great booby, of kind that isn't made any more, unless they're ordered from the seminary, and the anticipated spectacle of the joys reserved for him turned his stomach in such a way that he renounced his hunting permit before even raising his rifle."

And while inhaling the odor of stem and sap rising from the Bartelasse, my friend Marius Laparède obliged me to admire, once more, the panorama of the river, and continued in the amusing accent of Avignon:

"As provincial types go, for you who collect them, the mother and sons Clapisson were true type-specimens. If you were local, I would tell you that the Clapissons were from Carpentras, and that would tell you everything, for no region produces people more narrow-minded. In any case, you know the saying:

Carpentrassians, makers of onions,
Are cuckolds from Vaucluse to Vaison.

"Such proverbs are the wisdom and the justice of nations. It rains like that on Carpentras, from the Camargue all the way to Lyon."

And when Marius had poured out in that aside his ancient Avignonian hatred of the rival town, the former capital of Venaissin, which has the honor of having sheltered a conclave and making a pope, he continued:

"So, the Clapissons were from Carpentras; they did not emerge from Jupiter's thigh, for their fortune, which was considerable, dated from a grandfather, Barthélemy Clapisson, a pig-breeder and shrewd money-lender, in

180

that he was in partnership with a number of local pork-butchers and did not place his best stock with them. But grandfather Clapisson had a long arm, and in those days, in the realm of Avignon, when one had the clergy up one's sleeve, it was as if one had the good God there . . . things haven't changed much since.

"He came along at a good time, and the soutanes helped him to amass his wealth. Having earned his sacks of coin, as he was a man of ideas, he had that of making his son presentable. He sent him to study in Aix and bought him an advocate's office here. So, the Clapisson son becomes a parishioner of Saint Peter. The Clapisson office was in the Rue Vice-Légal, and the family still lives in an old town house of the era of Clement VI, which hasn't budged. The Rue Vice-Légal is the saddest and coldest in the city, it opens like a ravine at the foot of the Tour Trouillasse, but to live there is already to belong to old Avignon. All the nobles' town houses huddle there like vultures' nests in the giant shadow of the papal castle. Without the sculptures on the balconies and doors, one might think them lairs; they're grilled, bolted and padlocked, true dungeons of the Holy Inquisition. And what hygiene! One freezes in the middle of August, and from October onwards pneumonia is lying in ambush there, coughing. More draughts blow there than on the bridge—which doesn't prevent all those old nobles from clinging to their old dwellings even more than to their eyes. They have their souls bolted to their stones and it required old Monsieur de Poujadour to be ruined by the Bourse in order for him to sell his house to Père Clapisson.

"That wily colleague nevertheless installed his son there; the clientele of the convents followed him. The curés of Carpentras had given the nod to those there. The Clapisson office became that of great successions, holograph testaments and interminable lawsuits instituted around heritages, the parlor where the redemption of conscience was cooked of old criminals terrorized by the dread of Hell and the hope of the afterlife of all devoted souls. Oh, how many families were despoiled in the Clapisson study! Everything prospered there, the business and the lineage, for Madame Clapisson, née Lagardasse, the daughter of a rich miller of Sorgues, gave her husband eight little Clapissons. God blesses numerous families. Those devout folk, one might think that they had nothing else to do!

"The proverb was only half-true for the Clapissons. They had eight children, but only raised three; the other five died like flies. All in all, given the faces the survivors had, the others did well to depart. If you could see those Lenten mugs, as long as a day without bread, as thin as candles, with stooped shoulders! They had neither torso nor kidneys. One got bored just looking at them. Oh, I pity their wives! And what's more, as cold as the bottom of a fishpond; one is thirty years old now and has never had an adventure, the second is in the seminary and the youngest wants to go into it. As for the eldest, the one that concerns us, merely for having seen, by chance . . . how shall I put it? . . . the honesty of his fiancée, he took fright and immediately renounced the marriage.

182

"And that was the Clapissons' misfortune, believe me! There's one syllable too many in their name.[1] And then, Maladies like no one! Until they were fifteen they wore earmuffs, mufflers, scarves and galoshes until after Easter. The mother sat on them; they were never allowed out alone. They were eighteen when Madame Clapisson still accompanied them and waited for them outside urinals—and it was necessary to see her, hackles raised like a hen in defense of her chicks, preventing people from going in after her sons! Anatole, Eusèbe and Robert were so impressionable that the presence of someone cut off their means. Can you see those sausages next to a woman on their wedding night? They had, moreover, been reformed. I've already told you: maladies like no one. Necessary that they go to the waters every year, one to Plombières, the second to Chatel-Guyon and the third to Vittel. Nothing functioned in those boys, it was too much or too little.[2] Now you're informed as to their temperaments.

"It was the eldest of those mooncalves, Anatole in person, whom Grandfather Clapisson had taken it into his head to marry with Mademoiselle Anaïs de Mourlane. One of the oldest families hereabouts, the Mourlanes, and not the most loaded, although in a good enough situation. He had not lost the north, Père Barthélemy, and from the depths of his Venaissin pork-

---

1 It is the first syllable that Marius considers to be redundant. *Piss* means the same in vulgar French as in vulgar English, and has as many insulting derivatives.
2 At the time when the story was written the mineral waters of spas were promoted primarily as laxatives.

butchery he knew what heading he was setting on his compass. He had enough millers' daughters and peasant daughters-in-law like Mademoiselle Lagardasse. His son, the advocate of the Rue Vice-Légal, had died there not long ago. He had also had his fill of those pettifogging métiers whose progeniture all have the appearance of ferrets and invalids; he had seen too much of those sausage-hangers of grandsons; he wanted other little Clapissons to have a very different look, a very different color, and also very different adventures; he had not practiced usury for thirty years just to produce priests.

"The Mourlanes served in the fleet, father and son; the grandfather had been a vice-admiral; the father had died in the colonies as the captain of a frigate; a great-grandfather, before the Revolution, had been the governor of Martinique: it was a well-known name in the navy. There was a Rue Mourlane in Toulon and a Villa Mourlaniou in the vicinity of Brest. On the death of her husband, Madame Mourlane had come back to live in the familial residence, situated in the Rue Dorée almost next door to the Hôtel de Noves, where Madame de Sade lived. Mesdames de Mourlane, mother and daughter, had an income of twenty thousand; the Clapisson wealth was calculated at two or three millions.

"Mademoiselle Anaïs de Mourlane had the eyes of a corsair's daughter. Père Clapisson was not worried about the children that she would give to his grandson. All the broadsides weathered in the Far East by her father and grandfathers, all the adventures in Italy,

Greece, Turkey and Spain lived during brief stop-overs by an ascendancy of navigators, and their most recent escapades, finally, in the hot streets of Toulon, Marseille and Cadiz, vibrated in the crimson pulp of a quivering mouth, the mobility of open nostrils and the agile flexibility of a young body always on the alert. Mademoiselle de Mourlane had a face of pale and mat warmth, gray eyes of plaintive and troubled water in the shadow of long black lashes, a downy amber nape and chestnut hair planted low in that nape, rounded hips, small hands and a turned-up nose.

"Although very severely brought up by Madame de Mourlane, Anaïs and her physique had something that startled Madame Clapisson somewhat, but the grandfather's will was inflexible. The old fox was too well aware of what there was to gain; he wanted to bounce little pirates on his knee.

"I shall not tell you that Anatole and his pasty face of a reciter of prayers delighted Madame de Mourlane and her daughter, but Eusèbe Clapisson was already in holy orders and Robert, the youngest, wanted to go into them. It was, therefore, three millions that Anaïs would have one day. Those are reasons that triumph over many resistances.

"Mesdames de Mourlane went into society. In order to please the Clapissons the mother and daughter renounced their relations. They also received on Sundays; their salon was closed and they consented to spend those bleak dominical days, so long to kill in the provinces, in the country, in farmhouse breakfasts or picnics on the grass, followed by insipid walks in single file through the woods and meadows, in the company of the terrible Clapisson family.

"Madame Clapisson, née Lagardasse, had retained from her peasant childhood a taste for country picnics. She was fond of baskets full of victuals prepared at length the day before, spicy braised veal, jellied chicken and crayfish in mayonnaise insinuated into cans, of crockery and cutlery piled in hampers in order to be unpacked noisily on the edge of some lake infested with mosquitoes, in the feeble shade of three dusty cypresses, during the most torrid mistrals and the most ardent sunshine. The Mourlane ladies had a horror of those chores, but Madame Clapisson loved them more than anything, and as good sons, Anatole, Eusèbe and Robert approved blindly of everything their mother liked.

"They spoke in unison in that regard, the two soutane-wearers, Eusèbe and Robert, and Anatole, giving the impression of being as frocked as his brothers in his long overcoat, all three of them thin, black and long. Madame Clapisson mère followed. The curé of the Cordeliers, Monsieur Lecardon, was often in the party, and sometimes also Monsieur Maturotin, Monsieur Clapisson's former head clerk. The Mesdames de Mourlane yawned for the sake of the three millions.

"It was during one of these excursions that Anaïs de Mourlane had the terrible misadventure that cost her the husband and the large fortune. It had been decided that day that they would go to visit a *manade*. A manade, in Provence, is the combination of large enclosures where young bulls are raised that are destined for the corridas: in sum, a Provençal Granaderia. It was only a very small manade, for the true bull-breeders are in the Camargue. Nevertheless, they piled into a brake and after the dust of eighteen kilometers of sunlit road they descended at the door of the farmhouse of Père Mistraïou.

"'Bonjour, Madame Clapisson! Bonjour Monsieur Eusèbe and Monsieur Robert, and Monsieur Anatole and the lovely demoiselle! This is your son's promise? What a darling beauty she is, a caress to behold!'

"The lovely demoiselle, who cared little for all these expansions, had withdrawn slightly to one side. She spotted a pathway, the green freshness of which tempted her, a little path between two elder hedges. But Anaïs de Mourlane had a red umbrella that day, and, similar in the light that traversed the silk to a beautiful pink rose open under a poppy, she set forth into the meadows, without thinking any evil.

"All of a sudden, there are heart-rending screams and the howls of a woman having her throat cut.

"'Oh my God! The poor demoiselle! Quickly, lads, the pitchfork and the trident!'

"Two young bulls, excited by the rutilant umbrella, have plowed through a palisade and charged her full tilt. The entire meadow trembles and resonates, hammered by their gallop.

"Anaïs, frightened, only just has time to climb a tree. She is nimble and agile, the admiral's grand-daughter. Aiding herself with a low branch, she has gained a higher one; the forked trunk has provided her with a seat, and, clinging to the savior apple-tree, she is shouting at the top of her voice, for the two bulls are attacking her refuge with all the impetus of their charge; every blow of the head shakes her and threatens her equilibrium.

"People come running, the farm-hands ply the whip, the fork and the trident; the two beasts attracted by the red rag gallop in another direction. People occupy themselves with rendering aid to the lovely demoiselle. The eldest son of the Mistraïous helps her down, but he is a clumsy fellow, hasty and without precaution. He goes too quickly, and Mademoiselle de Mourlane's skirts remain hooked on a branch. Her dress makes a tulip, the muslin of her underskirts erupts like an inverted lampshade, and in her near-fall her bloomers are ripped . . . and all the assembled Mistraïous and farmhands, drovers and oxherds, are witnesses to the nudity and the shame!

"The three Clapissons, Anatole, Eusèbe and Robert, are also witnesses, as are Abbé Lecardon and Monsieur Maturotin, the advocate's former head clerk.

"'Oh, my sons!' cried Madame Clapisson the mother, opening noisily, between her progeniture and the disorder of her future daughter-in-law, the black taffeta of an umbrella that would not have excited the bulls.

"The Clapisson son withdrew his request and the Mesdames de Mourlane lost three millions thereby."

TAS-DE-FOIN

"HEY, have you heard the news?" said La Roche-Hébert, installing himself in the box next to mine at the Tower concert. "Poor Boisdory, croaked! The telegram arrived at the Club an hour ago. It's Luzarches who opened it at eleven o'clock. Edgar has taken leave of the go-betweens and the women."

"They weren't able to extract the bullet?"

"Yes—Trélat did the extraction yesterdays, but tetanus set in immediately, and tetanus is a matter of twenty-four hours. The poor devil died morphinated, numb. They softened, as much as possible, the final agonies. Thirty-five, full of vigor, a bachelor with an income of two hundred thousand . . . consequences of a hunting accident, a stray bullet! How that encourages you to go running after red deer and wild boar!"

"And in the family too; it was at his brother-in-law's that the accident happened?"

"Yes, out there at the Pontfermeux, at Ormettes. They're in consternation out there."

"Then Pontfermeux inherits?"

"Certainly he inherits—which is to say, his wife; this will permit those poor Pontfermeux to come back and live in their town house in the Avenue Fernand. They were badly hit in the last crash: there's a stray bullet that hasn't doomed everyone!"

"Oh, I see where you're coming from. Are you like that abominable Lormeril, the hardened skeptic who claims that it wasn't an accident?"

"God preserve me! But by nature, I believe in incidents."

"You exasperate me, my dear, you and yours, with your atrocious mania for wanting to unearth infamy and Machiavellianism everywhere. Why not the court of the Borgias right away—or that of the Valois, or even the Élysée, with nocturnal attacks and pillages of houses à la Portalis?"[1]

"Oh, if you're talking politics and displacing the question . . . "

"I'm not displacing anything . . . but pardon me. here's Camille Stefani! Look at that Stefani for me. Is she tempting and modern enough, that little primitive Italian maiden? Personally, I only come for her . . . and it's hard to come every evening, to study, for barely a quarter of an hour, a café-concert ingenuousness! But look at those wide eyes, almost naïve, the hair parted

---

1 The lawyer Jean-Marie-Étienne Portalis (1746-1807) became an important maker of legal theory after the Revolution, and had a crucial influence on the law of warfare, in what became known as the Rousseau-Portalis doctrine (although Rousseau had nothing to do with it), which limited but did not obliterate the right soldiers had previously had to pillage the property of non-combatants.

over the forehead, scarcely wavy, of Princess Madeleine, and the reserved curtsy of a little schoolgirl about to pronounce her compliment to Madame! Full of surprises! A little Eve, ripe to crunch!"

And La Roche-Hébert, very lit up, aimed his opera glasses at the little star with the floral eyes who, more provocative this evening than usual, with her Saint-Touch-me-Not grace and candid ignorance, had just come on stage slowly, her pretty head and delicate profile slightly inclined over her left shoulder: timidity of touching abandon?

Oh, that infantile and savant moue! Oh, that fashion of showing her neck and its whiteness by tilting her head like that, that Stefani, star of tomorrow!

Her appearance had electrified that early September hall, already crammed—as fashion dictated—with clubmen and boulevardiers.

A stir was produced at that moment in the hall. Heads turned, opera-glasses were adjusted. La Roche-Hébert's binoculars also followed the new direction of gazes, and then returned to Stefani's leotard, leaving to the curiosity of idlers their new target.

A tall, slightly plump brunette woman had just installed herself in the first forestage box on the right, and, smiling with strong and very red lips, her teeth short and very white, giving little nods of intelligence to the right and winks to the left, making a tour of the hall with a probing circular gaze. A name ran around, whispered from mouth to mouth, between the rows of the orchestra stalls. *Lady Naymore! Lady Naymore!*

191

The brunette now deployed a large red tulle fan with enormous anemones on each branch, and then, leaning backwards, took a blonde tortoiseshell lorgnette from the hands of a man in a black coat sitting behind her and started to study Stefani in her turn.

"La Djora," I said to my neighbor, for I too had recognized Lady Naymore. That pink camellia complexion, those large, moist velvet eyes, like black plush in the bistre of their rings, the strange bruised eyes of a lubricious slut, out of place in the calm freshness of the virginal face, I had known for a long time. They were very particular to her, that complexion and those eyes; although she had the delicately ridged and precise profile of an oriental Greek, her dimpled chin, her delicate nose, with mobile nostrils, and her short little teeth, like as many grains of rice in the moist fresh redness of her mouth, the redness of the interior of a fruit.

"Yes, La Djora, or Tas-de-Foin,[1] as we still call her," purred La Roche-Hébert, "Tas-de-foin, former mistress of a night, now a duchess and peeress of England. Is she still pretty? Yes, she defends herself. But it's free for you to judge her, my dear, you've only glanced at her."

"Is that the Duke of Naymore, the man accompanying her?"

"No, the Duke lives in Florence; she's making use of her pension of a hundred thousand francs a year and wears the title of Duchess; it's a bargain, that's all. Lord Westland, Duke of Naymore, has only ever laid a hand

---

1 This unflattering nickname means "Haystack." It does not appear in the original version of the story, "La Femme au tigre," as published in *Le Journal*.

on his lady peeress once in his life, at the high mass of his marriage—for Naymore is Catholic and Irish. He lives out there with Madame Daumières, the beautiful Madame Daumières, the wife of a banker whose separation caused such a scandal six years ago—she's been Lord Westland's mistress for eight. Tas-de-Foin maintains the household at a distance, and she has no lovers: that woman with the head of a sensual and chaste odalisque has always found sex tedious and tiresome. Now that her fortune is made she reposes, she's honest; it enchants her to sleep alone.

"I know a charming story about La Djora, from the days of her liaison with poor Alfred Dominger—Freddy, as we call him. Judge for yourself: Freddy, who fatigued her with the gluttonous and never satisfied passion of a voracious consumptive, began to cough and shiver seriously. I was dining with them that evening in the Rue Monceau. In the evening, the physician alerted by Tas-de-Foin, coming in consultation, took Freddy's pulse, made him stick out his tongue, ordered a diet, and worse, all diets. But Freddy pulled one of those faces, the face of a spoiled child deprived of dessert . . . and the appeals of his desperate glances in the direction of his mistress were touching and grotesque.

"When the doctor has gone, Tas-de-Foin rings; her chambermaid arrives. Tas-de-Foin gives orders: 'Quickly, make up a bed for monsieur in the guest bedroom, and a fire, and take this prescription to the nearest pharmacy immediately.' Then, with the satisfied sigh of a woman too tightly strapped up who has just removed the wounding corset: 'Mariette, remake my bed too, with clean sheets—fresh sheets my dear,' she whispered in my ear, 'sheets that don't reek of a man and all his villanies; it's three months since that has happened to me . . . how I'm going to sleep tonight, my little Roche-Hébert! If you knew, if you only knew, how amour bores me!'

"Well, fundamentally, that 'how amour bores me' is the story of Tas-de-Foin."

"Very nice, her 'how that bores me,' but what happened between you and Tas-de-Foin? You haven't saluted one another, nor exchanged a glance—not a movement of your lorgnette in the direction of the beautiful Lady Naymore."

To which La Roche-Hébert replied: "The fault of an opinion of mine. What do you expect? I told you. I made the mistake of not believing in accidents."

"What do you mean by that? That poor Freddy didn't die of consumption?"

"Freddy, certainly, Freddy died of Tas-de-Foin and several others. Phthisis in his marrow, he burned life and life burned him. A moth of bright celebration, he roasted his wings, and the rest, on as many candles in taverns as alabaster night-lights in tariffed alcoves. Anyway, Freddy died just in time; another year of that fine existence and he'd have woken up ruined. Now, La Djora wouldn't be the Duchess of Naymore today if she'd held on to Freddy. But there it is; you don't follow the English newspapers, otherwise you'd have read about the dramatic accident that happened in Bombay nearly two years ago to the English vice-consul, Lord Archibald Seener."

"What accident?"

"This. Lord Seener, six times a millionaire and the owner, in the vicinity of the city, in the middle of a forest of palms, of an old Parsee palace of which he had made a residence, had, like many of his compatriots installed in India, acquired a taste for and the habit of wild beasts. The interior courtyard of the habitation, paved with mosaics and florid with cacti, a veritable Indian Alhambra, had two tigers and three young lions roaming at liberty around a fountain. In the midst of those domesticated, growling beasts, there was a woman. A native? No, but worthy of being born there: the rosy and charming body of an indolent creole, with large eyes with bistre rings and a moist dark gaze: Lady Seener, or, rather, a fake Lady Seener, living there, invisible and reclusive, in that old rajah's palace, making no attempt to mingle with European society, not seeing or receiving anyone, a veritable odalisque, vegetating there, amid the cacti and wild beasts, her idle and monotonous seraglio life. That fake Lady Seener, you have divined, was La Djora, Tas-de-Foin.

"Where had Lord Archibald Seener encountered her? It doesn't matter; at any rate, he was madly in love with her! That tall, plump and idle whore has always strangely dominated the senses of the men who have possessed her. In brief, Lord Seener had taken her to India with him and installed her in the interior of that pagoda, in the midst of those monstrous flowers and wild beasts at liberty. She led the improbable and luminous life there of an enchanted princess.

It was in that magical décor that the terrible drama burst forth, two years ago, about which the English press talked so much. Lord Seener was found one morning, lacerated and bloody, the bones in his neck crushed, in the middle of the patio, killed by one of the two domesticated tigers. Who had opened the cage in which all of that menagerie was locked during the night?

"Lord Seener left by testament the four millions of his patrimony to the present Lady Naymore. Did La Djora have knowledge of that testament?

"Sympathy would clarify that doubt. Exasperated by dolor, La Djora, that calm and apathetic woman, had the five wild beasts of the menagerie killed that same morning by indigenous slaves, without a movement of pity for Nubian, the black tiger, her favorite, whose bloody claws designated clearly enough the author of the murder.

"Nubian had conceived, it has been said since, a veritable passion for Lady Seener. You're opening your eyes wide: it happens! The crime of bestiality is foreseen by the casuists; an animal can love and desire the amour of a human being. Lionesses have been seen in love with their tamer, and tigers mewling and gasping while crawling at the feet of beautiful female tamers.

"How do these monstrous passions develop?

"In general, it appears, it's necessary that it is us who make the first advances; the owners of menageries have, I'm told, sure means of degrading wild beasts! Balzac did well to write *Une Passion dans le désert!* Had La Djora read Balzac, and did she know those practices? At any

196

rate, in the low people of Bombay, where the passion of the tiger Nubian for his mistress was known, there were whispers about a drama of jealousy and amorous murder.

"Not that I accuse La Djora, but La Djora was bored and I don't believe in accidents. Anyway, without Lord Seener and Nubian, Tas-de-Foin wouldn't be a million-aire or a duchess today, and you wouldn't be admiring, in the heart of modernizing Paris, a woman who might have the blood of a tiger and a murderer in her veins."

FLOWERS OF SUBURBIA
(The Fortifes of Old)[1]

P ARISIAN suburbia and its sad surroundings! It has
always moved and charmed the sensitive and the
delicate; it has had its poets and attracted novelists. By
turns it has seduced Victor Hugo, the Goncourts and
Sainte-Beuve; more recently still, François Coppée and
the subtlest of our prose writers, Joris-Karl Huysmans,
have celebrated it amorously, also caught by the pitiful
charm of its ragged landscapes and desolate plains, the
charm of nature, sickened and debilitated, in a corner
of the Bièvre or the end of a plain in Gobelins, where a
poor street of an outlying district, with bed-sheets and
underwear hanging out of the windows, comes to die
outside the fortifications.

---

1 "Fortif" was a popular contraction of "fortifications" in the
days when the residues of the defensive structures in question still
marked the limits of Paris proper, separating the city from the
suburban districts; the wordplay involved in the feminization of
the term extends to the whores who haunted the fortifications at
the end of the nineteenth century, making use of the ditches for
swift encounters.

Melancholy and sly suburbia, always ugly and yet captivating with its ugliness of a suffering being, whether it is called Vanves or Gentilly, les Quatre-Vents or la Glacière, whether it has for a horizon the despairing view of the tanneries or the chimneys of Grenelle that extend along the bastions of the Route de la Révolte, and the red-painted hovels, *Sautéd Rabbit, Beer and Wines*, of the Barrière d'Italie, as if smeared by equivocal dregs of blood or wine, or the formidable and grandiose mud of Bicêtre, its aspect is the same everywhere. Among other poets of that skinned and weeping nature, Huysmans, in his *Croquis parisiens—Le Bièvre, Vue des remparts du Nord de Paris, La Rue de la Chine*—has described it too well, that flora of shards and rubble, its peeled huts, its sleazy sheds and tartaric buildings of clay and bricks, for me to waste time trying to depict after him all that suburban heathland, full of slag and plaster, and sown, here and there, with rotten fruit, ash and puddles, its strange soil inseminated with old newspapers and producing oyster-shells.

It is not only rotting straw mattresses and rubbish-heaps that grow there; between a leather-dresser's cage and a hill of tan-bark where a chicken is pecking, an equivocal idyll sometimes flourishes, simultaneously brutal and unhealthy, an idyll of an army whore and a soldier of the line, a handsome idler and a wretched maidservant, reaching its conclusion, for the girl, in a knife-thrust if she is passionate, and if she is venal at the Tenon hospital, around an exhausted, gasping hysteric whose insidious accomplices make her agony sing—and there you have two novels by the Goncourt brothers: *Fille Elisa* by Edmond, and *Germinie Lacerteux* by Jules and Edmond.

More often the idyll is an oarystis, and that oarystis a fine crime: the great city that tips all its refuse there exhales a breath of liquid manure that corrupts the marrow and the soul. In those lost corners, along the ramparts and the Voie de Ceinture, at nightfall, when the worker is asleep, his head in his hands, like the bank and its leprous grass, the peevish prowler and pimp wakes up; the mocking gamin who cried the program of the Buffalo yesterday, and today that of the Plaza, at the Porte Maillot as soon as the gas is lit, takes his first steps in the shadow of thickets, toward Fresnes or Poissy, and indifferent client of Cythera or Sodom. As for the streetwalker who goes before us, wiggling her rump and making her high-heeled ankle-boots ring on the pavement, when night falls, she turns robber and cut-throat.

The suburban streetwalker, the prowler of the fortifs! The Bois de Boulogne and the Bois de Vincennes become, when darkness falls, the rendezvous of all errant vices, all follies and all lusts. If the Allées de la Muettes and the ditches of the fortifications could recount the odyssey of all the cadavers found hanging from the trees in the avenues, and lying in the mud of the ditches!

Ask at the Court, the police station and the Prefecture about the frightful and constant role played by the prostitutes of the waste ground and suburban roads, the merchants of amour of the quarries of Issy and the abattoirs of La Villette, in the statistics of murders and thefts, their contribution to the great Book of Crime.

201

In Monsieur Macé's criminal museum[1] her name is Hortense Louet, she is the heroine of the affair of the Tour Malakoff.

Before the war, that tower, felled by Prussian cannon, was a country rendezvous where there was dancing on Sundays. Built at the gates of Paris in1855 by Monsieur Chamelot, the former restaurateur of the Rue Dauphine, it was the Robinson of Vaugirard and Montparnasse.

On the twenty-seventh of August 1876, the wife of the warden of the tower, a woman named Peltier, sixty-four years old, disappeared; on the twenty-eighth, her body was found at the bottom of a well. The victim's husband observed that her rings, ear-rings and watch had been stolen.

Suspicion fell on a man named Albert, twenty-five years old, a part-time bricklayer but primarily a pimp, and the prostitute Hortense Louet, his mistress, whom the Peltiers had charitably allowed to sleep in one of the ruined rooms of the tower.

The investigation lasted ten months without result; it was about to be suspended when, on the first of June, the murderer turned himself in. He wanted to avenge himself on his concubine, who, after having driven him to commit the crime, had abandoned him for another lover.

Louet, aged thirty, was arrested, and Albert put the responsibility for the crime on her; interrogations and

---

1 Gustave Macé (1835-1904) amassed a large collection of evidential items while head of the Sûreté, during the early days of forensic science.

evidence established that they had drawn their victim into the cellar on the pretext of searching for some lost rabbits; it was there that the defenseless Madame Peltier was strangled; as she was not dying quickly enough, Albert had smashed her head on the ground.

On the fifth of July, Georges Duval, an expert architect commissioned by the court consults the plans of the cellars and wells, and observed, in accordance with the indications furnished by the accused, that the cadaver of the Peltier woman had, with the aid of a rope passed under her armpits, been dragged for a distance of thirty meters through a narrow passage between twenty-five and ninety centimeters wide.

The two wretches, by reason of the sinuosities of the terrain, had harnessed themselves to the rope and had taken it up three times in order to avoid the fall of the body to the bottom of the ravine to the left of the path. When she was arrested, Louet had the victim's chaplet on her person. It was her who had linked Albert to the crime, saying: "In war, one kills!"

A flower of suburbia.

A suburban flower of the same family as the whore Louet, the sinister streetwalker of the Port Bineau, is the one known as the Singe-Vert, who murdered one night, in the company of three pimps—Liénard, Ferdinand and another who remained unidentified—a petty employee of indirect taxes, attracted by her to the bottom of a ditch in the fortifications.

"Playing hard" is the locution employed by that fine society for coups of that sort; at nightfall, the whore lies in ambush, indolently, on the round path; with a carnation in her lips, lifting up her skirt over her white stockings, she swings her rump and hips slowly, aiming at passers-by the sudden flash of her underwear, revealed in a savant movement.

There is a smile, a wink, a little *psst* . . . and if the mug advances, the Singe-Vert plunges stealthily into the thickets that descend into the ditches. The client, generally a petty rentier or employee, forced by economy only to approach the Cythera of the poor, sometimes an anonymous vicious wealthy man fond of the spice of base prostitution, is accosted and engaged by the whore, taken by her a little way from the road or the pathways of the Bois; the woman's pimps, following the phases of the adventure from a distance, having advanced for their part, tighten the circle stealthily and, at the desired moment, fall into the middle to the intrigue, and *go, lads!* The unfortunate fellow, belabored by blows, stunned and robbed, is left for dead on the ground. The unconscious man sometimes comes round an hour or two later, reanimated by the chill of the night and the keener air of the wood; glad to have got away so cheaply, he gets up and limps home, without daring to make a complaint. His case is not admissible: in the open air, an attempt on modesty . . . his conscience is not very clear, and then, perhaps he is married? Twenty times out of thirty the victim does not talk.

Impunity is therefore almost assured to the Singe-Vert and her two accomplices—and then, is not Morality on their side? In case of pursuit, they are protecting the modesty of the dryads of the wood. But when the fellow has the poor taste not to escape and adds one corpse more to the list of the "stiffs" of Parisian gallantry, the case for the Singe-Vert and her worthy acolytes becomes more serious. The Prefecture does not joke with cadavers; on that occasion, the law owes society a condemnation; it is then that, in the argot of the Singe-Vert and her friends of both sexes, it "smells bad" it is "going to spoil," and they reproach one another furiously for having "done a fine job."

In any case, there is no shortage of fine work in the ditches of the fortifications: it rains knife-thrusts and cadavers there; there is the little old man of the Porte Bineau, found literally assassinated at the foot of the rampart, the client of the Singe-Vert killed by Ferdinand and his mate Liénard; there were the bodies of the two ironworkers from Montparnasse picked up, riddled with stab-wounds, at the foot of the same fortifications at the Porte de Vanves.

They did not have sixty years between them, those ironworkers. Comfortable artisans, earning six or seven francs a day, both tall and handsome lads, but idlers, running after women like all umarried workers in the outlying districts, regulars of the drinking-dens in the Rue de la Gaité and the Théâtre Montparnasse, they must have got involved at the fortifications, far from policemen and busybodies, in a brawl commenced in a ballroom around some dancer's skirt, at the wine counter, or a game of Zanzibar:

> The tankards were empty
> And they were about to go . . . a roll of the dice
> Was to determine the night of the beauty

And who would remain, led to the quarrel.
. . . They went out to chat with no candle . . .
. . . .
All ten of them came to the foot of the stairway
And charged . . . Damn, what a clash of steel!
I had a heat in my heart . . . the girl, half-dead,
Shouted "Help! Murder! To me! Lend a hand!"

The scene is the always same: whether or not the Singe-Vert (the Singe-Vert is in all the suburbs, at the Porte Bineau as at the Porte de Vanves, the Route de la Révolte as at Montparnasse) witnessed the battle ignited by the odor of her skirt or the coins in her woolen stockings, the following morning, the two ironworkers were found, riddled with stab wounds and "carved up" in the fatal boundary ditch.

One of the two victims, Jules Polzien, was still clutching a handful of red hair in his fingers. In the spasm of death, his hand had closed convulsively on the head of his murderer and had not let go. The other victim, picked up still breathing, expired the following night in the hospital, without having been able—or rather without having wanted—to pronounce a name.

The Sûreté organized multiple raids in Montparnasse, Grenelle and elsewhere, and there was terror in the clan of thieves. Anyone with a murky conscience and red hair trembled in thinking about the terrible lock. A fête in Vaugirard, which was in full swing, was suddenly depopulated, and wrestling matches took place between banquettes, and for good reasons. One evening, in the

Place Cambronne, the police collected suspect blouses and jackets like strawberries in a wood.

A precious indication: the streetlamps around the scene of the murder had been extinct. Might the brawl have begun as a fist-fight, and in the obscurity, had two combatants, sensing themselves to be weaker, drawn and used their knives?

A mystery!

The police asked questions and found nothing. Suburbia has a prudent discretion regarding crimes and quarrels; loose talk can lead so far!

Some time afterwards, at the Barrière de Fontaine-bleau, the cadaver of a young workman, twenty-three years old, almost a child, was picked up in a Gentilly clay pit, the head almost buried in the moist, soft soil of the quarry. The wretch had been smashed over the head; when information was sought, opinion immediately designated a digger, Victor Demay, alias Bébé, thirty-two years old, a close friend of their victim.

Here, amid the rude odor of slaughterhouses, the flower of suburbia mingles with the sinister reek of an idyll of the prison camp, one of those unisexual idylls such as were seen blossoming in the lax age of Greece, the cruel and corrupt empire of which even the mild Virgil did not disdain to sing:

Formosum pastor Corydon ardebat Alexin.[1]

---

1 "The shepherd Corydon burned with passion for pretty Alexin." From the second Eclogue.

A strange affection linked those two men, it appears: an admitted and recognized affection. The night preceding the crime they had spent together in the lodgings of the murderer. At dawn, the older, returning to his work as a digger, took the younger to the quarry and, seized by some hysterical and jealous fury, killed him with a blow of a pickax.

Doctor Lombroso,[1] if consulted, could have delivered the key to that enigma of mystery and blood.

The flower of suburbia.

This summary of a rather bloody week can prove once again that it is not only old beggars carrying barrel-organs and the phantoms of white horses in fenced pastures who wander the uncultivated suburban heaths before the distant cupolas of the Panthéon and the Val-de-Grace, rounding out in two violet balls against the crumbling mist of clouds, everything down below, beyond the circular railway, of tall factory chimneys and the leprous slopes of the fortifications.

---

1 The Italian criminologist Cesare Lombroso (1835-1909), the founder of the pseudoscience of criminal anthropology.

AN OLD STORY

Then Herod, when he saw that he was mocked
of the wise men, was exceeding wroth, and sent
forth, and slew all the children that were in
Bethlehem, and in all the coasts thereof, from two
years old and under, according to the time which
he had diligently inquired of the wise men.

(*Matthew* 2:16)

AND having put his elbows on the table, Narzens
began:

"It was four or five years ago, well before the scandals and the transparent chronicles regarding Monsieur Auguste, Madame Pygmalion and Princesse Alphonse, well before the public adventure of Garanger and Petite Ordure and the war of knives waged by the ghouls of Lesbos against husbands and lovers.

"Poor Mizy, who subsequently became Mendès' *Mephistophéla*, was then neither the morphine-addict nor the wretched lunatic over whose agonizing fantasies and a few thousand francs—the last alms left to a phantom of a woman by creditors and businessmen—

the demoiselles of the building were fighting like stubborn crows over a living cadaver. Mizy was then only a very disquieting and very slender young woman with the impertinent head of a boy and the sparkling wit of a street-urchin, whose pretty quips, of an admittedly cynical and refined corruption, were causing a stir in the boudoirs. There was the: 'Oh well, the kid was boring me and I've unhooked it,' explaining summarily a miscarriage following a riding accident; and then the: 'My husband only loves me as a boy,' given as an excuse for the mania for masculine fashions she had definitively adopted; and finally the famous: 'What are you complaining about? I'm not a child!' brazenly responded, in the presence of the commissaire, to the unfortunate marquis who had just broken down a restaurant door without being able to have a legal adultery observed—the whole string of words of a similar ilk forming a prelude to the terrible: 'My brother and I have had the prettiest women in Paris,' which was to lead to the fatal divorce proceedings and close to the list of the marquise's worldly *concetti*.

"So, it was five years ago, or six, or more; the entire population of Veules was disturbed by the arrival in the streets of the village, at a rapid trot, of a landau with four powdered lackeys and postillions, and the presence in that landau of four pretty young people—very, very pretty! Shiny eyes, feminine complexions, teeth of a young wolf, short curly hair, small hands, small ears, strange gazes and even stranger smiles.

"The landau stopped—do you now Veules? Yes? Oh well—shortly before the little bridge of the mill,

210

a hundred meters below the Villa Meurice. The doors opened, and our pretty young persons leapt down; it appears that those messieurs were women: men from the waist to the hair to judge by the tight jacket, the pinned plastron and the felt hat; women from the waist to the feet, to judge by the pleated skirt, the silk stockings and the delicate footwear. They were the marquise, Princesse Katte Anska, her inseparable companion, Violetta Smunok, the pretty Dutch actress, than a boarder with Monsieur Perrin, now of Monsieur Clarétie,[1] plus one unknown to society, since reentered into normal life, having fortunately remained anonymous. Those ladies were in a symmetrical party, two couples of turtle-doves come for a little excursion from Paris-Mytilene to Veules-in-Lesbos.

The marquise, camped before the villas, her monocle in her eye, had soon reconnoitered the terrain. A good quartermaster, she had soon discovered a very suitable "To Let" up above, on the cliff, whereupon she started climbed the stairway in that direction, with her squadron following on her heels.

"'How much for a week, your hovel?'

"'My hovel? But Madame . . .'

"'Pay no attention—manner of speaking, just my way. Yes, how much per day? To be paid whenever you wish?'

---

1 Émile Perrin was the director of the Comédie Française from 1871 until his death in 1885, when he was succeeded by Jules Clarétie. This contention made sense chronologically when the original version of the story appeared in 1887, less so when the revised version appeared in 1911.

"'But Madame, I only let it for the season, and . . .'

"'How much for your season?'

"'Three thousand francs.'

"'Less dear than by the day; would you like two thousand francs for a month?'

"And the two banknotes emerged from a card-case stuffed pell-mell with banknotes and cigarettes.

"And that evening, my friends! What a spectacle, what a blowout! The table set outside, on the terrace, in the open air; the gardens of Veules, ravaged, had provided the flowers, the Hôtel des Bains the dinner, all the champagne and shellfish, and well! there were cries, café-concert refrains and ticklish laughter, and gusts of tobacco and kisses: a true fricassee of muzzles and cigarettes.

"The tenants of the neighboring villas, climbing on balconies, or ladders applied to walls, could not believe their eyes. The Manche itself, moved to joy, had taken on before that little feast a false appearance of the Ionian Sea. The evening concluded with a descent into the village and a stroll of the ladies through the unique street. All four linking arms, cigars in their mouths, singing at the top of their voices a then-fashionable chorus:

> *Emile,*
> *Is never in the dark;*
> *He always hits the mark,*
> *Emile!*

"The next day the scandalized owner gave the ladies notice

212

"'Why? The neighbors are complaining? No means of loving, then? It embarrasses them, poor cats! Why look? Let them plant trees! Anyway, I've had enough, I'll go. Don't weep, darling, my little Violetta, don't worry. I'll send for your mother.'

"And with that, an abrupt departure, in the marquise's landau, of Princesse Katte and the unknown, and the following day, the arrival of Madame Smunok, urgently, from elsewhere, for she was visibly suffering, the little Dutchwoman. Every day, her delicate elongated face of a brunette Jewess was getting thinner and deteriorating further. Since the departure of her friends she had abandoned the jackets and the false collars; she was in long and mobile foulard dresses and lace, and she spent her days henceforth, lying on the terrace in the thin shade of tamarisks, ripening in the hot August sun a pregnancy ostentatiously reaching its term.

"Here, I'll let the good countrywoman speak who was summoned to the villa to look after the invalid; the worthy creature, in her peasant simplicity, recounted everything without reflection, malice or artificiality, and as such, her story is quite gripping:

"The pretty lady, who was about to give birth, so becoming and so gentle that one might have thought her a holy Virgin, was in bed in her room, with her mother beside her, who was, in my opinion, a very worthy lady and respectable too, and also the mossieu, who was the doctor that the two others brought with them from Paris in the morning.

"The other, the little blonde, who seemed to be leading everyone, had an esphysiognomy that wasn't decent, and, God forgive me, argued like a man, with unchristian clothes, was in the next room with the other lady, arrived with her in the morning, fat and flabby, heavily made up, and didn't have the air of anything good.

"The weather that night was a pig, with gusts of north wind and rain, rain, as they said in the region in the old days, to sell the head of Robillard's doll. The sea was growling like a nasty beast, but fortunately, there were no boats out that night, that's for sure . . .

"So, as I was saying, it was blowing and raining, and the little blonde woman, who hadn't wanted to go to bed, because the pretty lady who was about to give birth and had never had a child was beginning to suffer, and we were already beginning to hear her moan, while the little blonde woman was pacing back and forth in the room, her hands in her pockets like a real man, and, excuse me, muttering between her teeth: 'Those pigs of men, you hear, Catau? Oh, the pigs!'

"The other one the fat one, who was slumped in her armchair, responded as if she were asleep: 'What do you expect, necessary to let nature take its course.'

"The other responded to that with nonsense, and kept on pacing back and forth muttering: 'Oh, the pigs, the pigs Oh, that kid! If I had it!' with a face so odd, so odd that I was almost scared.

"Then, suddenly, in the next room there was a scream, but like the scream of an animal being killed; my blood took a turn . . . then the door opens and the doctor calls and says: 'Hey, the nurse!' I run forward, and even bump into the blonde woman, who had also bounded from her place like a cat.

"The bed was full of blood and so red one might have thought that a veal calf had been bled, and in that red the pretty lady was lying, all white, as if she'd fainted. Next to her was the mother, who was holding the newborn child the *poulot*, in its wrap.

"Then the doctor comes in, to tell me to wash the child and have the linen warmed, and to go in quest of hot water. I almost lose my head; I confide the *poulot* to whoever, to the blonde woman . . . at any rate, after an hour, or half an hour, the woman in bed, changed, warmly wrapped up, wakes up, having drunk her warm wine, and I think about the child, the poor angel, I can no longer hear it whimpering.

"'Where's the *poulot*?'

"'Next door, with the Marquise.'

"The Marquise is the blonde woman.

"I go in . . . no light . . . like a gust of cold wind . . . rain and wind wetting my whole face; I hear very clearly someone closing a window, and when my poor eyes can see in all that dark, what do I see? Standing in front of the window, with the child in her arms, the little blonde woman, but the child all unwrapped, stark naked, its poor little head tipped back, mouth open, poor little cat. There was a moonlight that night by which one could see as in daylight the sea raging under the cliff, and under that moonlight, which was falling from directly above, she had such a funny look, the marquise, that I suspected a trick, and I almost threw myself at her to take back the baby. Poor little thing, it was all cold, all cold and all wet; cold and wet too, the hands of the lady, as if she'd come from outside.

"She didn't say anything to me; which didn't prevent that the little one died the next day of a fluxion of the chest.

✳

"'I've never read crime stories in the feuilletons, Mossieu,' the good woman added, 'but holy Virgin, that night, when I saw that blonde lady with her poisonous face, standing in front of that window, holding that poor innocent, all wet and all cold. I've reflected very often since that I'd lived an hour of my life in one of those stories. Then, there was a terrible sea that night, all white like milk under the moon, that the wind was raging under the cliff, a wind of Robillard's doll!'"

"And was the child a boy?" someone asked the storyteller.

"Naturally," replied Narzens. "The Amazons only suppress males."

A PARTIAL LIST OF SNUGGLY BOOKS

G. ALBERT AURIER *Elsewhere and Other Stories*
S. HENRY BERTHOUD *Misanthropic Tales*
LÉON BLOY *The Desperate Man*
LÉON BLOY *The Tarantulas' Parlor and Other Unkind Tales*
ÉLÉMIR BOURGES *The Twilight of the Gods*
JAMES CHAMPAGNE *Harlem Smoke*
FÉLICIEN CHAMPSAUR *The Latin Orgy*
FÉLICIEN CHAMPSAUR
   The Emerald Princess and Other Decadent Fantasies
BRENDAN CONNELL *Clark*
BRENDAN CONNELL *Unofficial History of Pi Wei*
RAFAELA CONTRERAS *The Turquoise Ring and Other Stories*
ADOLFO COUVE *When I Think of My Missing Head*
QUENTIN S. CRISP *Aiaigasa*
LADY DILKE *The Outcast Spirit and Other Stories*
CATHERINE DOUSTEYSSIER-KHOZE *The Beauty of the Death Cap*
ÉDOUARD DUJARDIN *Hauntings*
BERIT ELLINGSEN *Now We Can See the Moon*
BERIT ELLINGSEN *Vessel and Solsvart*
ERCKMANN-CHATRIAN *A Malediction*
ENRIQUE GÓMEZ CARRILLO *Sentimental Stories*
EDMOND AND JULES DE GONCOURT *Manette Salomon*
REMY DE GOURMONT *From a Faraway Land*
GUIDO GOZZANO *Alcina and Other Stories*
EDWARD HERON-ALLEN *The Complete Shorter Fiction*
RHYS HUGHES *Cloud Farming in Wales*
J.-K. HUYSMANS *The Crowds of Lourdes*
J.-K. HUYSMANS *Knapsacks*
COLIN INSOLE *Valerie and Other Stories*
JUSTIN ISIS *Pleasant Tales II*
JUSTIN ISIS AND DANIEL CORRICK (editors)
   Drowning in Beauty: The Neo-Decadent Anthology

www.ingramcontent.com/pod-product-compliance
Lightning Source LLC
Chambersburg PA
CBHW050301110726
47898CB00007B/2488